THE MISALLIANCE

THE MISALLIANCE

PANTHEON

BOOKS

NEW YORK

ANITA BROOKNER

All rights reserved under International and Pan-American
Copyright Conventions. Published in the United States by
Pantheon Books, a division of Random House, Inc., New
York. Originally published in Great Britain as *A Misalliance*
by Jonathan Cape, Ltd., London.

Library of Congress Cataloging-in-Publication Data

Brookner, Anita.
The Misalliance.
I. Title.
PR6052.R5816M57   1987   823'.914   86-42980
ISBN 0-394-55340-3

Manufactured in the United States of America

ONE

Blanche Vernon occupied her time most usefully in keeping feelings at bay. In this uneasy month of the year – cold April, long chilly evenings – she considered it a matter of honour to be busy and amused until darkness fell and released her from her obligations. These obligations were in any event minimal, but being self-imposed were all the more rigorous: no one else sustained them. Not quite a widow, and therefore entitled to none of the world's consideration, she bore her divorce nobly but felt its shame. I am innocent, she felt like proclaiming on particularly inclement days, and I always was. My husband left me for a young woman with a degree in computer sciences and in whom I can discern not the slightest spark of imagination. As this event baffled her, she felt humbled by it. Thus humbled, baffled, and innocent, she felt all the more need to hold her head high, to wear a smile that betokened discreet but amused interest in what the world had to offer her, and to complete her toilette, down to the last varnished finger-nail, before leaving her house every morning.

Leaving her house – in reality a tall brick building containing several mysterious high ceilinged apartments – was the event of the day, after which she felt she could breathe more freely, having launched herself yet again on the world without meeting any resistance. Her steps were brisk although her destination was a matter of some uncertainty.

5

The Wallace Collection knew her, and the National Gallery, but not the British Museum, where she had once felt faint, or the Victoria and Albert, where she had had an alarming prevision of extinction between two glass cases containing Mosan metalwork. She was subject to these irrational feelings, largely concerned with her own end, and needed to summon up a particularly quizzical tolerance in order to keep panic at bay. Her neighbours thought her unapproachable and therefore did not approach her. This did not amaze her for she was so intensely occupied in her attempt to resolve inner contradictions that she rarely noticed the signals she gave out. Many a time she had remembered a face and had smiled, too late, and the smile had faded slowly, to be replaced by a look of sorrow. That too faded slowly, more slowly than she knew.

Her husband, Bertie, had left her after a marriage of twenty years, and those twenty years were never absent from her consciousness. She had been very happy, but she supposed that he had not. She had, in those days, felt such energy that she had obliged herself to be less exuberant than she might have been, thinking such exuberance an embarrassment in one who was still uncertain of pleasing. She therefore cultivated tastes which she felt instinctively to be thin, sharp, brittle, like the very dry sherry which Bertie assumed that she liked as well as he did. She was thus always ready with bright conversation for him, as they drank their sherry, full of anecdotes, for she had observed him to be uneasy with anything more subjective, expansive. The need for anecdotes had led to that multiplication of activities which was now standing her in such good stead. Voluntary work at the local hospital fed her seriousness, although what she brought home from those afternoons was more often than not amusing. She thus became what is known as a conversationalist, and always remembered to order more sherry. After his unfaithfulness her husband preferred to

6

think of her as a cold woman, although he knew that she was not. Sometimes he still visited her in the evenings, calling in on his way home. Blanche always kept a few varieties of light discourse on offer, much as she kept certain stores in her cupboards. But these days she drank wine, rather steadily.

She maintained an excellent appearance, not so much because she valued such excellence as because she could thus use up much superfluous time. She calculated that she could spend up to an unwanted hour every morning by simply putting herself to rights, and producing a pleasing effect to lavish on the empty day. She took no pride in this, although she might have done; such altruism, such meticulousness is in fact heroic. She saw no heroism in it, but merely a form of despair; the mornings were a bad time for her. Something about the grey London light, bright yet sour, as it entered through her tall windows and intensified the pale walls of her large rooms, kindled an habitual feeling of uneasiness, as if only in the coming of such sunshine as she could remember or imagine would she relax. The sun is God, said the painter Turner. In the uncertain light of these uncertain days, her thoughts turned to images of an illusory but brilliant heat, the sky turned to whiteness, the air dry and filled with scent, the whine of a passing vehicle receding as the afternoon emptied and discouraged movement. She thought of the evenings of these imaginary days, the sun intensifying into redness, the sky cooling to a light bright green, and then to a white that seemed laid over indigo. And of the nights, balmy enough to encourage open windows, late music, the drifting smoke of a last cigarette, sheets cool and dry to welcome the still-warm limbs. But, as it was, she had only these April mornings to work with, chilly, light, unwelcoming, waking her too early, launching her into the day too soon. And so she lingered in her bedroom, and chose her armour with care.

7

This image of the hot day began mildly to obsess her as she walked through the studiously dim rooms of museums in her tweed suit and polished shoes. Sometimes she cast about with rather more assiduity than usual in an attempt to find an image that would match her fantasy. But the images before her eyes presented too much in the way of otherness, brought with them a freight of references that she felt unable to pursue; the skies were either too bland or too stormy, the foliage too alien, the colouring too mild for what she had in mind. Rendered mentally helpless by the half light of those empty days and by the long grey afternoons, she sat on many benches and looked at many pictures. What she saw was not represented on any canvas but was a kaleidoscope of fragments, possibly once seen and quite unconsciously retained. These fragments, apparently disconnected, and with little relevance to her present circumstances, seemed to possess a certain authority, since they came unbidden. She saw a window opened on to a dazzling garden; some sort of tea party, the sun glinting off a silver teapot. And then again a garden in the early morning, with water drops sparkling on the heavy heads of lilac, a cat running fastidiously through dewy grass. And then a white chair and table in that same garden, with Sunday newspapers discarded and ready to be taken inside. This last image she recognized. It was at his mother's house, she thought. It was when we were engaged. It was when I took Bertie's tea out to him in the garden. A conscientious woman, she then reproached herself for indulging in personal reminiscence when there was so much for her to admire on the walls of the gallery. She did not expect art to console her. Why should it? It may be that there is no consolation. But, like most people, she did expect it to take her out of herself, and was constantly surprised when it returned her to herself with no comment. The smile of certain nymphs seemed almost to mock her as she finally stood up to go, and their plump arms seemed to usher her, with much ceremony, from the room. For this reason she always felt slightly reduced by the art of the past, rebuked for her mildness, scorned for her seriousness. The past had its secrets, which she sought very much to know. The National Gallery frequently challenged her assumptions, which was her reason for returning. There was even something contingent in her faintness in the British Museum, where, surrounded by acres of frozen Greek marble, she had been transported in her mind back to a disappointing holiday in Greece; then, as now, strolling through the museum, she had come up against the archaic smile of the kouroi, votive figures who seemed to contain an essential secret knowledge that had always escaped her. Their smile, like that of the Goddess with the Pomegranate in Berlin, pertained to certainty, to fulfilment. Because of this she avoided all echoing spaces, all confrontations with images of festivals from which she felt herself to be excluded, all mysteries which she could only dimly apprehend. This was not simply timidity. It was perhaps the fear of the infidel, neither pagan nor Christian, but it was also awe, the proper emotion to be felt. If she were to be admitted to these mysteries, then they would be revealed to her. It seemed to her that she had only to wait. Nevertheless, she sought instruction, hoping for a sign, hoping to do better. The National Gallery she considered the definitive factor in her faulty education, and she went there two or perhaps three times a week.

After these visits, the return to the unenlightened life of her more than ordinary day was difficult to negotiate. She addressed herself to the business of shopping, of buying an evening newspaper, of preparing her return. Still conscientious, she shopped scrupulously, testing everything for freshness, regretting that she was too disciplined to buy great quantities, indulging vast imaginary appetites, piling tables with profusion. But she restrained herself, for on whom

9

would this waste be wasted? Instead of the street markets of her fantasy, she was confined to the bleak neon radiance of a single store. Her polished shoes carried her among well-trodden ways, and finally to the bus stop, outside Selfridges, where she came momentarily to rest. Fragments of other lives surrounded her, other conversations, American, Arabic, Italian, French. A long queue of schoolchildren lounged against the plate glass window of the store, arguing, drinking orange juice out of bottles, wearing baseball caps back to front. They looked hardy, confident, up to date. At the bus stop two dark-haired women, arm in arm, complained loudly to each other about a third. A large bearded man, wired up to headphones, was silently but energetically stretching the fingers of his left hand, as he jabbed the fret of a phantom guitar. Elderly, tired, and overdressed, the widows of the neighbourhood emerged from gloomy flats for their afternoon stroll; Blanche saw stark and heavy colour applied to sagging cheeks and lips, patent leather shoes crammed on to plump and painful feet, hair golden and unnaturally swirled and groomed. Blanche watched a woman wearing a heavy fur coat feel for the edge of the pavement with her stick; a scaly hand, ornamented with long red nails and an accumulation of rings, emerged from the weighty sleeve like a small armadillo. She felt terror for this woman, as she imagined the painful process of dressing up, of assembling the attributes of wealthy old age in emblematic and unsympathetic fashion, much as those nymphs in the National Gallery, with their pearls and their golden hair, their patrician smiles, had carried their freight of attributes to mock her present condition. But the nymphs had mocked her own exclusion from their world of love and pleasure; the widows mocked, like the fates, unconsciously, indifferently, but with a sense of foreknowledge: you will come to this. You will be like us, unpartnered, still fashionable, doughty, stiff of body and sad of mind, obstinate, tough, liable to blame everybody else, our daughters-in-law who do not telephone us often enough, our grandchildren, who, although adored, are incomprehensible, the porter of our expensive block of flats who fails to bring up the laundry, the hairdresser or the manicurist who plans to take an inconvenient holiday. Blanche, who had neither diamonds nor fur coats nor daughters-in-law, regarded these women studiously, empathizing all too accurately with their stoical disappointment. Beneath the golden hair, their ancient eyes stared back without curiosity, all fellow-feeling long gone, half-heartedness still whipped up into some sort of discipline, expectations very low. As the sun made a brief appearance, the over-painted lips smiled, revealing the ghosts of girls long gone. Then the sun disappeared again, leaving only the ordinary day behind, and all the expressions resumed their habitual air of resignation.

The person on whom Blanche would have liked to have lavished all this alternative waste and profusion (for waste was as illusory and haunting as the absent sun) was no longer there, and there was no family for whom she might have liked to prepare meals and treats. The only child of parents long since dead and almost forgotten, Blanche had begun her apprenticeship of living alone from an early age, and was thus an expert. An expert is not necessarily contented with his or her expertise, and Blanche found her skill sorely tried as the days grew longer. Her marriage had been a source of amazement to her because there was always somebody to talk to. At the beginning she had talked too much, too artlessly. Novices in love think they have to explain their childhoods, recount their entire history up to the moment of meeting the object of their choice. And they do not learn from the fact that this process may have to be repeated. Blanche, although innocent, had learnt her lesson quickly, and had come round fairly soon to the sort of impersonal conversation that her husband most enjoyed. Like many rich men, he thought in anecdotes; like many simple women, she thought in terms of biography. He called her fanciful but was at one time proud of her. He liked to travel, to beautiful and fashionable places, and while he looked up old friends in these places she wandered through the towns, by the shore, lonely and content, knowing that he would be there when she got back. When they met again in the evenings, in these fashionable and beautiful places, she would try to tell him of her simple enjoyment, her solitary cup of coffee, her walk in the public gardens, or some conversation she had overheard. But he was impatient with this, and had much to tell; his information was full of incident, as if his friends, like himself, had more staccato lives, faster, more eventful, more objective. It was then that she had learnt to tailor her conversation to his requirements and to those of his friends; she was not calculating in this, but simply wanted to please. And she succeeded admirably, for his friends, who were not quite hers, found her rather amusing. As she was habitually elegant, she passed muster very well. But she always thought back to the early days, to her breathless welcoming of him in the evenings, her dashing to the kitchen to bring him a taste of something she had prepared that afternoon for dinner, and to what he called her romancing. Her transformation into the controlled and quizzical creature she had become had been effected on the whole without pain. It was her husband who had fashioned her into the woman she was now, so independent, so dignified, so able to manage on her own.

The images of waste and heat came together suddenly in her mind as the bus rounded Hyde Park Corner: a market in the South of France, and bushels of plums releasing their scent in the hot sun. A stallholder had stuck a carnation into the apex of the pyramid of fruit, already spoiling, moist, blackish pink, overripe. She had bought some of the plums and they were soon oozing through the bag. After inhaling their smell, which was almost of wine, she had thrown them away.

Her smile careful, her mind elsewhere, as it so frequently was these days, Blanche greeted a woman whose face was familiar to her and made her way to the platform of the bus. Trying to place the woman took no small effort, simply because of the unwieldy furniture in her mind. The woman's smile had been so warm that Blanche supposed they knew each other quite well, were neighbours, in fact, and that it was only her increasing preoccupation which forced her to reconstruct the woman so laboriously. From an image of anxious brown eyes and a pretty concern for others she arrived at the conclusion that this woman, as well as being an acquaintance, was known to her in some professional capacity. Doctor? Dentist? That was nearer. The face had been bent over some sort of ledger or appointment book in the image that now came into focus. Of course, the dentist's receptionist. Mrs Duff, the dentist's wife, who helped out with great pride when the regular receptionist took her holiday, and who, when not at Harley Street, was Blanche's neighbour, an inhabitant, like herself, of the flowerless streets of West Brompton.

Phyllis Duff: a good woman. The picture was now clear. Excellent wife, devoted companion. Keeping up to date, up to scratch, planning her wardrobe – modest but superior – with due care but little conceit. Always presentable, in the old fashion of the wife of a professional man, usually to be found in her spotless home. Mrs Duff had no pretensions to be, nor could she ever be mistaken for, the new breed of woman who takes on the world. She had the brilliantly cared for appearance, the fine stockings, the rosy silk scarf, the first-class handbag, of the woman who dresses for a day in town, emerging a little hesitantly from the stony fastness of her mansion flat, looking at all the shops but returning home only with some lampshade trimmings. A woman, in

13

her own and her husband's eyes, of some importance, with sacred rituals: my quiet time, my day for baking, my evening for the League of Friends, my spastics. A woman preserved from another time, smiling trustingly and confidingly, given to pleasantries of a bland and custom-worn nature, lacking in surprises. Blanche reflected on the wholesomeness of Mrs Duff, her extreme remoteness from the world of business activity, from the technological expertise, the sheer boldness, of Bertie's new friend. Like the virtuous woman in the Old Testament, Mrs Duff supervised all the goings out and the comings in. Her husband, when he left in the morning, knew that when he reached the end of the street, she would be standing at the window or on the little balcony to wave, following him with melancholy brown eyes. And that when he returned in the evening it would be to a warm kiss and the aroma of a serious meal. Blanche, unwrapping a Dover sole from a paper that managed to be both dry and glutinous, imagined Mrs Duff at her preparations, the gleam of her immaculate kitchen, her gravity, her expertise, her peaceful anticipation of the evening's reunion. Her wifeliness, so out of date, so infinitely beguiling.

Stirred to something approaching restlessness or vivacity by the very fact that the day had been partially conquered, Blanche wondered if Bertie might look in on his way home. For this reason she took a bath early and dressed in a white silk shirt and a patterned velvet skirt that she knew he had once liked. He was disappointingly vague about colours and tastes and might not even remember it, she thought. She tried to remind herself how inadequate his responses had been after all those sense impressions she had tried to ply him with. She could hardly believe how drained of them his day might be, although he himself did not seem to feel the lack.

'What did you have for lunch?' she would ask him eagerly.

He would appear to search painfully in the recesses of his

memory. 'Meat,' he would say finally. Or, 'Some sort of fish.'

Moving now with some purpose about her kitchen, she took another look at her sole, found it dispiriting, and put it at the back of the fridge. She would cook it later, for she was conscientious about her well-being and thought it poor-spirited to descend to the sort of food that people tend to eat when they are alone; bits of cheese and fruit and the ends of anything that had not already been eaten. She liked to set a table, even now, and did so as if, were she to be surprised, all would be in order, civilized, devoid of self-pity. Even after a year of this kind of life she still thought in terms of Bertie's calling in, as sometimes he did; she did not care, out of pride, out of love, to cause him any of the uneasiness she was almost sure he must feel. She took out a bottle of Vouvray, nicely chilled, and put it on a small silver tray with some very thin dry biscuits. That was what her shopping was best at these days.

The dull but harsh white light of a sunless April evening, with a hint of damp in the air which turned the pages of the evening paper limp, and the unrelieved green of the garden beyond her window, caused a spasm of physical chill which she counteracted with her first glass of Vouvray. The evening, if Bertie failed to come, did not look promising. All she could expect would be a telephone call from her sister-in-law, Barbara, a few letters to be answered, some sort of music on the wireless, and then the order of release: bed. How is it possible, she thought, pouring herself another glass, how is it possible that my life has slipped through the net in this way? It is true that I have only been on my own for a year and am still a little shaken; perhaps I shall get used to this ... inactivity. For she felt herself to be inanimate and did not know that many people feel like this, men as well as abandoned women. But she knew, without a hint of sentiment, that her life might just as well be over, and although she had stared so recently at that image of Bacchus and Ariadne in the National Gallery and had willed that ecstatic moment of recognition into being – so immediate that Bacchus' foot has not had time to touch the ground as he leaps from his chariot, so shocking that Ariadne flings up a hand in protest – nothing now would happen. The greyness of the sky would permeate her evenings and her days would be spent in unrewarding schemes of sustenance and improvement. But she was in need of the unwilled action, the bonus, the discovery that would bring back into her veins the warmth of that illusory sun that had shone for her once and whose whereabouts she could not now locate. Scanning the empty sky from her window, and hearing the last car of the returning wage-earners being parked in the street below, she sighed and thought that Bertie would not come now.

The telephone rang: Barbara. The two women had remained on good terms after the divorce, for Barbara, a more sardonic version of her brother, had always regarded his activities with some scepticism. When he had introduced his sister to the computer expert with whom he had fallen in love, Barbara had remained unimpressed. 'You want your head examined,' she had said to him afterwards. This had not gone down too well, for Bertie had always needed his sister's approval.

'Amanda is all I ever wanted,' he had replied. 'We fell in love almost simultaneously. She has given me a new lease of life.'

'You mean she's twenty years younger than you are,' said Barbara, unmoved. 'And what are you going to do about Blanche? She was all you ever wanted once.'

'Blanche has become very eccentric,' he replied.

This was pretty well undeniable. Blanche went to such lengths, thought Barbara, always dressed to the nines, making elliptical remarks that no one knew how to take. Always carrying on about characters in fiction, or characters whom she said should be in fiction, and sipping uninhibitedly from various bottles of wine. But one couldn't deny that she was a first-class wife, although less interesting and open-hearted than she had been when Bertie had first brought her home. And a woman who bore no malice, taking all the blame. She had simply bowed her head when Bertie told her that he was in love with this Amanda, or Mousie, as he uningratiatingly called her. Bowed her head and said, 'Do you want me to move out?' Even Bertie had been uneasy about her humility, which was entirely genuine, and had rather sharply told Mousie they must look for somewhere to live: Blanche would remain where she was. Mousie had thought this a rather foolish idea, and so, in many ways, did Blanche. She had no desire to remain in the flat and had thought of living abroad, but she forced herself to stay because she knew that Bertie wanted to be generous, and she had not the heart to disappoint him.

'The least he could do,' said Barbara, who, like Bertie, misunderstood the situation. 'And is he making you an adequate allowance? He is not a poor man, Blanche. I hope you are not being foolish.'

'I was not foolish enough,' said Blanche mournfully. 'I suppose that he got bored with my being sensible all the time.' Barbara privately thought that Blanche was very far from being sensible, at any time, but she let it pass. 'It is far too late to be foolish now,' Blanche went on. 'Besides, I have money of my own. I don't want any more.'

Barbara had sighed, had taken a closer look at Blanche's thin face, and had been moved to something like compassion.

'Perhaps you'll marry again,' she said. 'You're quite a young woman. And still good-looking.'

She did not say, 'How will you live now?' But that was what she meant, and they both knew it.

'I shall be fine,' said Blanche, with one of her intimidating smiles. 'I am thinking of joining the Open University. Or finishing my thesis on Mme de Staël. There will be plenty to keep me busy. I shall do a Cordon Bleu cookery course.' 'You are a very good cook, Blanche,' said Barbara. 'Don't be silly.' 'I have always been interested in archaeology,' Blanche went on repressively, for matters were threatening to get out of hand. 'Something entirely new. There will be no time to be bored. Besides, I have always despised women who say they are too frightened to live alone. There is no room for that kind of woman in this day and age.'

Barbara, who knew that Blanche was precisely that kind of woman, had since made a point of telephoning every evening. As they understood each other perfectly, neither made any attempt at serious conversation.

'Am I disturbing you?' Barbara would say. 'Are you alone?'

'As it happens, I am,' Blanche would reply, in a tone that indicated surprise at this turn of events. After which exchange comments would be friendly, ruminative, neutral, for each had an interest in keeping the tone light. They were united in having too little to do and in their desire to make the best of it. They felt humbled and disturbed by their old-fashioned immobility, aware that they were out-moded, almost obsolete. Despite their many voluntary activities, they felt unworthy. They looked out with wary but not uncritical eyes on the changing moral landscape, and consulted with each other on matters of no consequence, having not quite mastered the art of declaring their dearest wishes and their hearts' intentions. Instead, they kept their secrets to themselves, and understood each other perfectly.

'How is Jack?' asked Blanche on this particular evening.

'A touch of gout. Temper not good, as you might have expected. And he insists on playing bridge tonight, with that couple next door. Well, it is our turn, I suppose, but I tend to forget about these things. Tell me, Blanche, how long do you suppose taramasalata keeps? I somehow can't bring myself to throw it away, although it looks hard round the edges.'

'When in doubt, throw it away. You're not feeding these people, I hope?'

'Well, just coffee and cake.'

'Quite right. Bridge players get so envenomed that I doubt if they will know what they are eating. It's really just something to break up the arguments, isn't it?'

'It probably will be this evening.' A pause. 'Any news?'

'No, no news.'

'You're all right?'

'Tremendous.'

'You wouldn't care to join us, I suppose?'

'It's kind of you, Barbara, but you know I don't play. I refused to learn when Mother kept bursting into tears and cheating. Such an atmosphere. The thought of it makes me feel quite ill, even at this distance. But thank you, all the same.' Another pause. 'Love to Jack.'

'I'll tell him. Until tomorrow, then.'

'Until tomorrow. And my love to you,' said Blanche, and put down the receiver. There would be no further calls this evening.

This is what they call freedom, these days, thought Blanche, as she grilled her sole. Freedom to please myself, go anywhere, do anything. Freedom from the demands of family, husband, employer; freedom not to pay social calls; freedom not to play any sort of role. And I daresay some people might want it, since it is supposed to be the highest good. That is, they might want it *theoretically*, but free will, I find, is a terrible burden. If one is not very careful, free will can come to mean there being no good reason for getting up in the morning, becoming ridiculously dependent on the weather, developing odd little habits, talking to oneself, and not having very interesting conversations with

19

anyone else. One's thoughts becoming self-referential, untranslatable. The world is not always waiting for one to discover it, particularly when one is my age: the world, that entity bandied about so frequently, is in fact an endless multiplicity of impermeable concerns. And myself with none of my own.

Slowly, thankfully, the day darkened into night. Rain had come on, as it always seemed to these evenings. The tyres of the very few passing cars hissed on the wet road. The sun is God, thought Blanche, pulling her heavy curtains.

Pouring herself another glass, she reflected that time had a different meaning when one experienced it on one's own. People talked such nonsense about human affairs, she thought. All this prurient concern with 'relationships', and the vast literature, high and low, that had grown up about them was really neither here nor there. Love – for that was what was meant – was like the patrician smile on the faces of those nymphs in the National Gallery, admission to the privileges of this world, arbitrary, unteachable, hardly a matter of reason or election. Love was mysterious and, for all the anxious speculation that had grown up in its wake, incommunicable. Love was the passing favour dispensed by the old, cynical, and unfair gods of antiquity; it was the passport to the landscape where the sun shone eternally and where cornucopias of fruit scented the warm air. But for those whom the gods disdained, and Blanche felt herself to be one of them, the world was the one after the Fall, where only effort and mournfulness might lead to a promise of safety, where sins would seem to have been committed without joy, where nothing gratuitous could be hoped for, and no lavishness bestowed, and where one's partner, one's referent, one's *vis-à-vis*, the mirror of one's life, had turned into an acquaintance of uncertain intimacy, whose conversation, once so longed for, was, more often than not, alien, uneasy, resentful, and boring.

Blanche, an inhabitant of that fallen world, prepared for the evening ritual of dispensation, for the lustrations which would at last leave her free to close her eyes. She ran her second bath of the day and poured into it an essence that smelled of flowers; conscientiously, she once more cleansed and tended the body which seemed to be holding up quite well, despite the various threats of disintegration that the day had held. Her face, in the clouded mirror, had the anxious look, the lugubrious bleached look, of an inhabitant of mediaeval Flanders. Carefully she washed away the day, brushed the hair, smoothed in what she thought of as embalming fluids. Below the long white nightdress, her ribbed Gothic feet shone palely. Thus prepared for her nightly journey into the unknown, the only journey which she did not fear, she stood for a moment at her window, the curtain held back in her hand. Over the dark and silent garden a silent cat stalked. The trees were motionless under their weight of moisture. From the sodden earth came an exhalation of damp. Hearing the owl, Athena's attendant, hooting in the far distance, Blanche let down the curtain, took off her robe, and went to bed.

TWO

Tuesday was Miss Elphinstone's day and therefore moderately populated. One day a week had been agreed on by both of them shortly after the divorce, when Miss Elphinstone had found Blanche waiting for her in a spotless kitchen and had said, 'Not worth your paying me for nothing, is it? I'll come in on Tuesdays and if you want me later in the week you can give me a ring.' Fear of being eliminated for ever from Miss Elphinstone's crowded life had spurred Blanche into disposing of the empty bottles and leaving a dirty cup and saucer on the draining board and an ungathered newspaper in the living-room on Tuesday mornings, thus implying a temporary neglect that would require Miss Elphinstone's crusading zeal and keep her there until lunchtime.

Miss Elphinstone seemed to enjoy a lively and dramatic existence lived in the shadow of some excitable church whose activities absorbed most of her time and whose members abounded in competitive acts of selflessness. Thus was ensured an avalanche of information that took up most of the morning. Severely hatted, and wearing an overall under Blanche's last season's black coat, Miss Elphinstone carried an equally severe black leather hold-all which contained a pair of rubber gloves, a change of shoes, and a religious magazine to read on the bus, although as she invariably noticed something of interest on the journey the magazine remained unread and was occasionally offered to Blanche, whom Miss Elphinstone considered to be in need of spiritual guidance. Retained not so much for her services as for her turn of phrase, Miss Elphinstone thought of Blanche as one of her parishioners but was sufficiently authoritative to refrain from forcing her hand. On arrival she would remove her coat, change the shoes, and sit down at the kitchen table for tea and biscuits. This she was clearly unwilling to do, preferring to stand in the doorway to deliver her monologues. Egress from each room in turn was blocked by Miss Elphinstone's figure giving an unedited version of the week's events, each one charged with incomprehensible significance. The cup of tea was Blanche's attempt to forestall Miss Elphinstone's colonizing effect on the flat. Being monosyllabic herself, Blanche considered that news, once delivered, was self-limiting. In this she was gravely mistaken, as she had reason to recall once a week. Miss Elphinstone, ennobled by words, demanded an isolated vantage point for optimum effect. She was contemptuous of the tea and biscuits, which she considered a weak civility characteristic of the bourgeoisie. She would sip disdainfully, while putting herself out to accommodate Blanche, in whose life she took a professional interest. Offhand questions were posed, details remembered. Her tone was critical, her agreement rarely offered. 'Been busy, I see,' she might say sardonically, nodding her head in the direction of a batch of waferish coconut biscuits. 'Coming round, is he?' she might ask, disguising her avidity with a barely assumed detachment. For Bertie, who had once brought tears of scandalized laughter to her eyes, she retained a fascinated respect. Like many blameless women, she loved a disreputable man.

This interlude over, she would carry the cups to the sink, and, donning her gloves, would turn both taps full on. Above the roar of the water she would begin her aria. A coach trip, of an ecclesiastical nature, had been planned to some outlying beauty spot, but this had brought complications in its wake. There had been an unpleasantness, Blanche might remember, when a newish member's offer to organize it had been turned down. In view of that trouble last year this came as a surprise to no one. There were various other hazards to be overcome, some of them of a psychological nature – Miss Elphinstone would not burden Blanche with the details. Allusions to this matter were guarded, but none the less forceful. Miss Elphinstone had taken it upon herself to proffer certain suggestions, which had not been too well received. There had been an exchange of views, some of them lacking in cordiality, but Miss Elphinstone had stood her ground.

'You see my point, Blanche,' Miss Elphinstone would say some time later, poised in the doorway of the dining-room. 'I'm in a trap of me own devising.'

Blanche would regret all this news as she later watched Miss Elphinstone putting herself to rights for the journey home. Over and above admiration for Miss Elphinstone's virtuous yet interesting life, she appreciated her extreme elegance. Miss Elphinstone had none of the waistless high-stomached appearance of the elderly, although she was of an age at which one is normally encouraged to put one's feet up. A tall pale woman, with abundant grey hair drawn back and secured somewhere in the recesses of her hat, Miss Elphinstone carried herself well and trod gracefully on her narrow and substantially shod feet. Blanche's black coat hung straight from her thin shoulders; Blanche's black and white silk blouse was concealed by a spotless if faded overall. The ritual whereby Miss Elphinstone smoothed and tidied her hair without removing her hat fascinated Blanche, and reminded her of convent girls taking a bath in their shifts or matrons undressing on the beach. Frequently Blanche would buy a garment which did not quite suit her but which she could see quite clearly on Miss Elphinstone. 'Well, I'll take it off you if you've no call for it,' Miss Elphinstone would say in a critical tone, her long dry hand lovingly feeling the material. 'I dare say I can get some wear out of it. It might do for the outing, if the weather holds. Though that's now in some dispute, as I was telling you. Well, yes, Blanche, if you're making coffee anyway; I've just got time for a cup. I hope you'll do some proper shopping this week. We're low on everything, I see. And I've defrosted the fridge, so you'd better not fill it up until later.'

Seated once more at the kitchen table, bag and gloves by her side, Miss Elphinstone would sip her coffee and look around with an appraising glance. Blanche would wait for some word of commendation, but, 'We thought of Bourton-on-the-Water this year,' Miss Elphinstone would say. And then, 'Thought about going away yourself? Why don't you ring up Mrs Jack and ask for a loan of the cottage? I hear we've got a touch of gout, so *he* won't be much in evidence. A bit of fresh air would put you to rights, if I'm any judge.' How Miss Elphinstone gathered her information was quite unclear to Blanche; she supposed that information, like some heat-seeking particle, flew to its natural home of its own accord or inclination. And Miss Elphinstone's tangential acquaintance with Bertie's sister entitled her to that form of patronage which implied a balanced and almost omnipotent weighing up of the evidence. She knew that Barbara and Jack Little possessed a cottage in Wiltshire, and she frequently assigned Blanche to a restorative stay there. But Blanche rarely went, impelled by sheer inertia not to move from the flat, a worrying trend of which she was increasingly conscious.

When the moment of her departure could no longer be delayed, Miss Elphinstone's procedure was always the same. She would give a final twitch to the curtains, tell Blanche that she found her looking peaked, remind her of the supplies she needed, and would finally close the door behind her. Out in the street, she would look back at Blanche who would be standing at the window, and would bare her brilliant false teeth in the sort of smile that betokens an impeccable conscience. Blanche would wave her hand until Miss Elphinstone disappeared in the direction of the bus stop.

In the new social uncertainty of her divorced state, in which, she had observed, she was to be left relatively alone so that she might 'find her feet', and presumably be returned to her friends as a person who would not give the lie to her former sophistication, rather than one who might rehearse her grievances at inconvenient moments and in civilized gatherings, Blanche was interested, but not surprised, to see that sympathy was on the side of the guilty party. The hubbub of speculation that surrounded her husband's new liaison had made itself felt even in Blanche's silent rooms. She was well aware that this speculation contained an element of the desire to see Bertie make a fool of himself or come a cropper, in which case the call would go out to her once more and she would be invited to give her opinion. It was even hoped, vaguely, that she might effect her re-entry into society by marrying again; but until then, she was, like certain Hollywood actresses in the bad old days, on suspension.

She gave so few signs of madness or rage that it was difficult to sympathize with her. Indeed, it was Mousie's contention, vividly expressed to her sympathetic friends, that Blanche had brought Bertie to the verge of complete emotional sterility by virtue of her 'intellectual snobbery'. This view had reached Blanche, as such views always will, and had met only honest bewilderment. She perceived the difference between Mousie and herself as a very simple one: Mousie was used to being loved. Metaphorically, Mousie had been holding out her arms, in the certainty of meeting a welcoming embrace, since she was a little girl. Even her nickname, Mousie, bestowed on her at that same early age, betokened spoiling, cherishing, a father's, if not a mother's, indulgence. By holding out her baby arms Mousie had emitted the correct signals: people knew what their response should be. And because she was so delightfully forthcoming, because she was so easy to understand, because she was so artlessly pleased with the response she invariably elicited, she was allowed to be equally artless when the response was perhaps a little lacking in fervour. Tears of rage would start up in her eyes, accusations would pour from her hotly, presents would be spurned. In this way she cemented attachment through guilt, and any discomfort that this might cause would be swept away by one of Mousie's lightning changes of mood, her gaiety, her demands for affection, of which she could apparently never have enough. Mousie needed to function from a position of emotional dominance; as this was an art which she had learnt in her cradle, and as it had worked so well at that time, she had seen no need to modify it throughout her adult life.

Bertie, used to the calm unemotional woman whom Blanche had become, had been enchanted by the petulance, the self-assurance, and the shamelessness of Mousie. He took all these qualities as evidence of passion, in which he was mistaken, although it was an easy mistake to make, and he was not alone in making it. Bertie himself, a rich man, of reserved and powerful personality, represented to Mousie the father to whom she could stretch out her infant arms once more, a delightful prolongation of her habitual and instinctive state. Bertie, whose desire for control was easily titillated by a token opposition, and who had begun to see in Blanche a strength of character that seemed to challenge his own, had succumbed easily to Mousie's appeal. Not for Mousie the discretion of a woman technically in the wrong; her very indecency had thrilled Bertie to the core. Mousie would telephone him at home, sometimes tearfully, if she had not seen him that day, and was not put out if Blanche happened to be at hand. Once Blanche had answered, and had said, 'Do you wish to speak to my husband or are you going to pretend that you have the wrong number?' This was taken by Mousie to be a massively unsporting response, and she had complained, with tears, to Bertie about it. Bertie, seeing vistas of unease opening suddenly before him, had also responded by blaming Blanche. In this way Blanche could be isolated by virtue of her innocence. The discomfort of the guilty parties could only be resolved by invoking Blanche's lack of co-operation. Behaving properly, in this context, took on a radically different meaning from Blanche's understanding of the matter, or indeed of any matter.

'Your little friend telephoned,' Blanche would say to Bertie, as he returned from the office, looking alternately younger and more harassed. 'Why don't you ask her round? I hate to think of her huddled downstairs on the doorstep.' For how could Bertie pretend to be faithful to Blanche when Mousie had made the facts of the situation so patently obvious? And how could Blanche, so schooled in good behaviour, win in a contest with a naughty child, with tactics long expunged from her life as stupid, dishonest, above all uncharacteristic? It was particularly difficult to behave with dignity in such circumstances; for in order to negotiate successfully, Blanche would have needed to transact in what she privately considered to be an unworthy manner, and would have had to call on reserves of patience and cunning in which she was notably deficient. It was all the more puzzling in that the baby whom she knew Mousie to be was disguised as a young adult woman who earned her living in an adult way and lunched in wine bars with her young upwardly mobile female friends, all of them busy gentrifying the south-western suburbs and comparing notes on their live-in companions. Marriage they scorned, thinking of it as the shackle that kept women at home, or at best tired out with being too successful all round, yet oaths of fealty were exacted, as in some new code of chivalry. Blanche, musing over a glass of wine and a sandwich, could see these lunches quite clearly. The talk would be excited, the briefcases parked on an empty chair; acquaintances would be hailed in delighted and uninhibited tones. And when the confidences started, the heads would be lowered and would come together, and the laws of the Mafia would prevail. Mafia honour must be satisfied, no matter what the price to be paid. In fact the price was always survival: no laughing matter, as Blanche had reason to reflect.

Naturally, certain rationalizations had had to be circulated before the divorce could take place. The most useful had been confided by Mousie to her friends. 'If the man decides to look elsewhere,' said Mousie, 'you can be sure that his wife can't satisfy him.' The friends all saw the wisdom of this. However Blanche's current isolation was caused not by the opinion of Mousie's friends, whom she did not know, but by the parallel defection of her own, all of whom seemed to think privately what Mousie and her friends were saying so publicly. Blanche's habit of arcane references, her way of raising unsuitable matters at dinner parties, thus came to be seen as evidence of thin blood, of reserve, or of incapacity; she was far less interesting than Mousie, who was so dramatic in her reactions. And it was not always clear what Blanche meant. If you had not read the same books you did not always make sense of her allusions. Whereas Mousie was a child in comparison, an adorable child. Tiresome too, on occasions, and embarrassing, but on the whole great fun.

'I see it all,' Blanche had said to Barbara, in the course of one of their less guarded telephone conversations. 'I am not adorable. I can be very sarcastic, and that is apparently more wounding to Bertie than the plain fact of Mousie's taking possession. And now people seem to think that I am frigid, and there is no possible way in which I can refute them. So clever of them, don't you think?'

29

'You could sleep with their husbands,' said Barbara, who was a plain-spoken woman.

'I only ever wanted to sleep with my own,' said Blanche sadly. 'And apparently that was wrong too. People would have been more sympathetic if I had had a messy and injurious private life. It would have been evidence that I am human.'

'Farmyard thinking,' said Barbara. 'I'm surprised you take any notice.'

'Ah, but my dear, I am meant to. And I think I must.'

'I really think that Bertie has behaved unforgivably,' said Barbara to her husband after she had put down the telephone.

Jack's response was to chuckle. 'I never would have thought he had it in him,' he said. 'Pompous bastard, I always thought. And he's come up with a little cracker like this girl. Bad luck for Blanche, of course,' he added hastily, seeing his wife's look. The matter had not been discussed again.

And so the word went out, as the word always will, that Blanche was to be the loser. And as curiosity had to be satisfied, Bertie and Mousie had to be invited to dinner. And as Mousie was adept at the business of survival, many allusions were made in the course of these dinners to Blanche's famous eccentricities. Thus the legend was established and the verdict was passed: Blanche was too eccentric to be borne. She was *insupportably* eccentric. And age could only make her worse.

Bertie, who thought his wife uncomfortable although he knew her to be honest, abstained from these colloquies, said nothing to refute the current or received opinion, but sometimes called in on his way home, or perhaps later, in the course of an errand to the off-licence. Carrying a wrapped bottle, he would observe, testily, that Blanche drank too much.

'What did you have for lunch?' Blanche would say. For

she was not surprised at the way things had turned out. If, as Plato says, all knowledge is recollection, she had always known that she would fail in this particular contest, for her own plainness as a child had caused her to look longingly at the delighted smiles bestowed on other, prettier little girls, and she had wished in vain to have a tantrum of her very own. But the tantrums of plain little girls do not have the desired effect, and by the time those plain little girls have grown up and become elegant women the art has been lost for ever because it has never been possessed.

And since then the weather had seemed to be uniformly awful, although Blanche was well aware that she was extrapolating from her own inner disarray. Nevertheless, she was statistically sure that somewhere there was heat, there was sunshine, and radiance, and that this happy climate was reserved for those who had the determination to seek it. For herself, the grey days and the endless afternoons seemed a fitting context for her present life, and sometimes she needed all her courage to leave the house, driven out as she was by the even greater horror of staying in. And as human contact seemed to recede from her grasp, she craved it all the more, although her cocked head and quizzical smile, assumed out of frightened deference to the gods, had driven many lesser mortals from her company.

Her fantasies, on which her lips remained firmly closed, and which she would have died rather than reveal, came dangerously near to the surface as she surveyed the sodden garden and stood at the window immobilized by a vision of an alternate life, the one she would have wished for herself had she been in a position to lay her case before some benevolent tribunal.

If only I could live in a real house before I die, smell lilac in my own garden. If only I could be married again, to Bertie, young enough to be confident, not middle-aged and wary, having seen too much. If only it were Sunday, in summer, just once more, and I were about to take our tea out into the garden. And if only there had been that pram in the hall that is said to stifle all creative endeavour but would have had the opposite effect on me. Our sons, our daughters, playing in that garden, shaking raindrops from those lilac bushes, stalking the cat. Always hot sunshine, in these imaginings.

And no shame in getting old, getting weak. Arm in arm, companionably taking a walk in that garden ... the children coming to tea, with their children.

'Perhaps you should have given him a child,' Barbara had once said, goaded to harshness by Blanche's passivity.

'Perhaps he should have given me one,' Blanche had replied, speaking for once bitterly, out of her greatest hurt. And there the matter rested. They had never referred to it again.

On this grey day, momentarily warmed by Miss Elphinstone's company and the evidence that perfectly sane people lived equally ruminative lives, Blanche determined to shop and to cook as if she were a normal woman with normal household concerns. She bought supplies that would see her through the week, in case – always the lurking fear – she was kept at home by illness, and on her return did some more baking. Her excellent cooking, in which she required no co-operation, was, had she known it, a further count against her in Mousie's circle, as was her small private income. 'These houseproud women wouldn't be so houseproud if they had to do a day's work,' Mousie would say in the wine bar, flushed with anger, her hair slightly untidy after an ideological lunch with the friends. 'I believe in *involving* the man,' she would add proudly, remembering Bertie with an apron over his business suit and the inordinate length of time it took to prepare a meal, there being so much to discuss and so many false starts to be rectified. Bertie seemed to thrive on it all. And then they were out so much, at those dinner parties which kept Mousie in the forefront of everybody's attention, in the position that she found most effortless and most congenial. When Bertie required her to give a dinner party herself, she ordered everything from a caterer and dressed up to the nines to compensate for the fact that dishes tended to emerge from the oven at the wrong temperature. Though she drank less than Blanche, she became much more animated much more quickly. Blanche, after two or three glasses, merely became calmer and displayed the rudiments of a sententious smile.

Bertie, looking in that evening, found her halfway through a bottle of Sancerre, calm in her white silk shirt and her patterned velvet skirt.

'You must spend a fortune on that stuff,' he said uneasily. 'And it can't be doing you any good.' He hated evidence of solitary habits, just as he hated the echoing silence of the flat, as he stood outside wondering whether or not to use his old key.

'Don't worry,' said Blanche. 'I have never been drunk in my life. You do not run the risk of seeing me hanging round a lamp-post with a riotous hat over one eye. I think you are frightened of my turning up at your house and making a scene. Bursting in on your guests while Mousie is dishing up the stuffed peppers. Having to be removed by men in white coats. Reduced to begging in the streets, asking passers-by for five pounds for a cup of tea. Yourself shuddering with disgust on the other side of the road. Anyway, I can afford it. That must be one worry off your mind.'

Bertie sat down in his usual chair with a slight sigh.

'I hope I find you well,' said Blanche, looking at him with an expression of some reserve.

Bertie appeared strange to her. Mousie insisted that in the evenings and at weekends he change into clothes that broadcast messages of youth and leisure. He looked like a child, Blanche thought. 'In any case, I think it behooves lonely women to take on the burden of the world's drinking,' she said. 'Curious verb, behooves. I behoove, you behoove. Or is it intransitive? You'll find a bottle of Malaga in the larder,' she added, seeing that, as usual, he was taking no notice. 'Or there's some Madeira, if you prefer it. With a sliver of Madeira cake, perhaps.'

Bertie ran a finger round where his collar ought to be. 'Home-made?' he enquired, remembering that he was wearing a polo-necked jersey.

'Naturally,' said Blanche, getting up and going out for the tray.

They sat sipping in companionable silence, while Bertie ran an eye over his former home. There was no doubt that this flat was more congenial to him than his new home, although the house agent had told him that prices in Fulham were due to go through the roof. When they did, he planned to buy something else; Mousie was all for keeping on the move, exploring new possibilities, getting to know new people. Eventually, she said, they would want to settle down and become part of a community. But there was no hint of mobility or change in Blanche's rooms, where the lamps were always low and where furniture stood, shadowy, in the half light. Blanche, gliding back from the kitchen, seemed to be moving soundlessly, her feet half hidden. An atmosphere of quietude surrounded her activities; in all their years together he had never known her to be unreasonable. When he thought about it, as he sometimes did, he realized that he had never really been put out by her bizarre notions, although he now supposed that they were more noticeable than had ever been apparent to him. Of course, he was sorry to have upset her, more sorry than he judged it wise to let Mousie know, but the great thing about Blanche was her self-sufficiency. What was more, he had never seen her cry, whereas Mousie cried rather a lot.

'This carpet is getting shabby, Blanche.'

'True,' she agreed; 'but it is so dark in here that you can hardly see it.'

This, coming from her, sounded almost like an accusation.

'There is no need for it to be so dim. I keep telling you to buy stronger bulbs. Anyone would think you liked sitting in the dark.'

'I should look rather foolish sitting here by myself in a blaze of light,' she said. 'Besides, I should notice the shabbiness of the carpet. No, this way I can prepare myself for a good night's sleep. The evening is the time for meditation. It is a fitting way to end the day.'

'What is the matter with you, Blanche?' he said impatiently. 'You are not becoming melancholy, I hope?' Or maudlin, he added silently.

'Me?' said Blanche, giving signs of a fearful animation. 'I am in simply splendid shape. There is no need to worry about me, Bertie. I am in better shape than you are. You are putting on a good deal of weight, I see. Have some more cake.'

Bertie brushed crumbs from the front of his pullover and reached for another slice of Madeira cake. 'I shall take it all off when we go on holiday,' he said, with some dignity. 'I shall adjust rapidly. We shall be swimming a great deal, after all.'

'Oh, really? Where will you be doing this?'

'Didn't I mention it? We are going to Greece. Next month, as a matter of fact. We have taken a villa with some friends of Mousie's.'

Then I can't expect to see you for some time, she thought, and was almost relieved that he had let her know, so that she should not stand at the window and wait for him.

There was never much to say on these occasions, although Blanche sometimes allowed herself the luxury of saying more now than she had done when she was married to him. His presence comforted her, and in a way he took some

sustenance from hers. Once in a while he would have liked
to have stayed and watched television, not saying anything.
But he usually stood up, with a small sigh, after about three-
quarters of an hour, kissed her absentmindedly, and left.
Locking the door behind him, as he instructed her, Blanche
would go to bed and, on those nights that he had visited
her, sleep.

There was no rancour in her towards Bertie. She looked
on him, as she had always looked on him, as a kind of
gigantic treat, a prize won in a lottery, something fortunate
and undeserved, and, because undeserved, all the more
pleasurable. She even understood his defection, for he was a
restless man and she had always dreaded boring him. Over
the years she had hidden her sorrows from him, and in doing
so had lapsed into odd silences: often Bertie wondered what
he had done wrong. And it was a matter of honour to her
never to utter a rebuke, although he would have welcomed
it. Thus she sent him off to his new life with a whole area
of normality stretching between them, untouched. She had
simply refused to discuss what he referred to as 'the break-
down of our marriage', since, as far as she was concerned, it
had not broken down. This refusal had led to such discomfort
that it was a relief to both of them when he left. And yet,
even after a year, and with all her deficiencies intact, she still
waited for him to come back, and he, perhaps, on odd
occasions, found himself returning to what he had to be
careful not to think of as 'home'. He was aware of his age,
and of hers. But Blanche thought of herself as no age at all,
as dematerialized, made hollow by his disappearance. It was
as if he had taken her entire history with him. Bertie, when
he looked in on his way back to Fulham, would be dis-
concerted to see how young she looked. It was only after he
left, when she was alone again, that her face saddened and
altered. But Blanche, who was not much interested in how
she appeared to others these days, scarcely noticed the change.

THREE

Blanche saw the child and mentally appropriated her before she knew her name: Elinor.

The child, dressed in pink dungarees and a pink anorak, with a wisp of her brown hair caught in a pink ribbon bow, was about three years old and not conventionally appealing. What was impressive about her was her extraordinary gravity, as she sat, pursuing a piece of cake with a teaspoon, in the little vestibule where Blanche was dispensing tea for the Outpatients, this being her occupation for two days of every week, although she usually carried out her duties on one or other of the wards, where she was known to, and liked by, the patients, who saw something quasi-professional in her indomitable smile and her tactful lack of false cheer.

Blanche's first thought was that the little girl must be a foundling; no normal child could sit so quietly in this unsettling place, without fidgeting, without crying, without staring, without protesting, yet she had none of the awful passivity that Blanche had come to recognize in children waiting to see the doctor, children too sick to play, to question, to assert their own pagan energy. This child looked perfectly well, but indifferent to her surroundings, as she sat with the composure of a small adult, imposing a sort of autonomy on the uneasy conviviality around her, ignoring it. Like a foundling, she appeared wise beyond her years, as if on a mission, needing no guidance or assistance, but rather waiting for the story to be unfolded. Her dreadful patience, as she pursued the piece of cake, instead of picking it up and cramming it into her mouth, gave Blanche a pang of mingled horror and sympathy, for she saw signs there of a determination to succeed at difficult tasks no matter how easy an alternative there was to be found.

So great was the child's degree of self-possession that Blanche would not have been surprised to find her unaccompanied, but eventually a cheerful red-headed girl, who had been in animated conversation with the blonde mother of a fractious baby, leaned over to her, and, scarcely noticing the effort that was going into the accomplishment of the child's self-imposed exercise, said, 'Want some more?' Ignoring the child's reply, perhaps because there was none, or perhaps because it was too late in coming, she transferred her cigarette to her left hand, dug in the pocket of her complicated and fashionable kimono coat for some money, sauntered over to the counter, and said to Blanche, 'Another piece of that. Oh, and I might as well have another tea.'

I would not let her have any more cake, thought Blanche. It is synthetic and horrible and will do her no good. I would let her have a banana and some fruit juice; she would find the banana easier to eat and it would be better for her. But she said nothing and smiled at the girl as she gave her her change, registering, as she did so, a disagreeable impression which she could not analyse although it was powerful enough to make her transfer her attention from the child to its mother.

Unlike the child, the mother was spectacular, vivid, obtrusive. The ichor of extreme and abundant youth and fertility made its pulse felt in the sheen of her skin, the coarseness of the red hair, the limbs swimming in their layered cotton garments, the small feet bare in their black leather sandals. An air of wealth surrounded her and glinted from the gold bracelets she wore on either wrist. The incongruity of finding such a woman in charge of so plain and serious a child worried Blanche, as if the woman, by virtue of her very contemporaneity, her involvement in her own passionate and desirable present, could not possibly give the child the attention it needed, as if, in the shadow of such a mother, the child had learnt, too young, too drastically, the lesson that some are born to bask in the attention of others while some are destined for a discreet position in the half-light. While the mother's every movement proclaimed her intense appetite for life, the child's eyes seemed to be drawn downwards, in eternal contemplation of the elusive piece of cake, which she would not abandon until she had mastered the art of successful capture; while the mother laughed in conversation with the blonde woman on her left, and rectified her bracelets, and examined a chipped red nail, the little girl continued to ply her wavering teaspoon, an expression of perfect gravity on her face.

What worried Blanche, in the anxiety she now felt as she followed the child's unvarying efforts, was that the balance of life was on the wrong side here, that the vitality was invested in the mother rather than in the little girl. For an odd moment it seemed to her as if the mother were actually younger than the little girl, and she wondered if that was why she had felt so decisive a reaction when she had first identified her. It was not that her behaviour was in any way tiresome or displeasing; it was in fact a relief to find the mother of so small a child, in so gloomy a place, laughing so naturally and so confidently. What disturbed Blanche was the curiously blind and undifferentiated smile that the girl turned on everyone, as if the smile were not so much a response to the smiles of others as a function of the girl's own progress, as she swung through the rows of chairs, her cup of tea and her cigarette held slightly outstretched, like a libation, and then Blanche saw what had given her that slight shock of recognition. The girl's expression was the

39

same as the expression of those nymphs who had seemed to mock her progress through the Italian Rooms of the National Gallery on long slow April afternoons. She had the smile of a true pagan. She would operate according to the laws of the old gods rather than huddle in the mournful companionship of the fallen world.

So disagreeable a realization – for it was stronger than an impression – caused Blanche to accuse herself of gross eccentricity. It was as if the sight of the woman and the reaction she had produced had brought out in Blanche the latent madness of which Mousie had implicitly suspected her and of which she had hitherto given no sign. The woman, or girl, for she could be no more than twenty-four or -five, had done her no harm, had addressed no word other than a request for tea, had swept her searchlight smile over Blanche's face without ill-intent, not seeing her because she had no reason to see her, taking Blanche's outstretched hand with the plate, the teacup, at face value, simply as commodities. It was not the effect of the girl's indifference that alerted Blanche (for why should she not be indifferent?) so much as the girl's lack of sadness at seeing her child in these surroundings. Blanche, who was used to Miss Elphinstone's pursed lips as she strove to conceal her disappointment when she found a stray empty bottle, could detect sorrow, could detect it a mile off, could detect it even in Mrs Duff, met on the bus or in the street, eyes widening in sympathy as she registered Blanche's stately and disarming progress, her elaborate stratagems for going nowhere in particular, could detect it in Barbara, with her laconic telephone calls. The gift of compassion is born in one or not at all; the artificial commodity, assumed or advertised, misses too many clues. Compassion acquired later in life might have murmured over the plight of the little girl; it would not have registered the odd dimension of the deep and unfettered optimism – almost a secret – of the mother.

Taking herself further to task, Blanche wondered why the mother should not be optimistic. The child did not seem in any way endangered, did not even look ill. Only her gravity was unnatural, and her silence; Blanche now realized that she had not made a sound. As the room emptied, and Blanche came from behind the counter to collect the empty cups, she hovered near the couple, curious to absorb more of their signals. The mother continued to smile, to smoke, to glance at her watch: evidently an appointment had been missed or had not been kept. Her eyes did not at any time engage Blanche but continued their sunny progress over tattered magazines or through the contents of her large shoulder bag. Several times she got up and went to the telephone in the corner to make a call. She gave the impression of being not so much in a hospital as in some sort of transit area. Her mild impatience, as she checked her watch, added to the suggestion that she was in an airport lounge. She looked ready to fly off at any moment; the child might have been brought along to say goodbye. The idea that it was the younger of the two who was the more grown-up deepened, as Blanche, lingering by the table, gazed into the little girl's face and found in it the entirely responsible expression of a tiny adult.

'I'm afraid she must be getting tired,' she said to the mother.

The girl laughed. 'Well, now we're here, we might as well stay,' she said. 'We were a bit late and they told us we'd got out of order and had to come back next week. But I know the doctor; he'll see us if I can catch him.'

'She doesn't seem to be at all ill,' said Blanche.

'She isn't. She's perfectly fine, aren't you, Nellie?'

'Nellie? That's an unusual name, these days.'

'She's called Elinor. And *I* don't think there's anything wrong with her. It's just that she doesn't speak,' said the mother, turning away to light another cigarette.

The implications of this statement registered less with Blanche than the fact that the child's name was Elinor and that it suited her. She was well dressed, although her clothes were cheap, cheaper than those of her mother.

'Was that nice?' she whispered to the child, taking away the plate with the still unfinished morsel of cake on it.

Sitting back, and placing her hands in the pockets of her anorak, the child nodded. So she was not deaf, Blanche thought.

'Is she your only child?' she asked, falling back on trusted formulae, aware of a need to know more.

'Well, she's not really mine,' said the girl. 'Her mother died when she was a month old. And then I married her father and took them both on.' She laughed, as if at the enormity of this, eluding or abolishing all the information that might have been included and was not.

Blanche felt humbled by evidence of such rapid thinking, such careless experience, such lack of hesitancy. There was no evidence in the girl of painful decisions, painfully arrived at: she acted as if such decisions had caused her no furrowing of her smooth brow, had been easy, had been almost fun. But it would be a mistake to judge her on this, she thought, for such decisions have to be made, and who but the strong can make them?

Seen close to, Elinor's mother was nearly a beauty. A collection of well-defined, even sharp, features had been harmoniously assembled in a small white face: the eyes, down drooping at the corners, were deeply set, the eyelids a colour between grey and bistre. Both the ears and the nose were shapely and finely cut; the mouth, like the eyes, drooped naturally, as if in fatigue or disdain, giving a hint of boredom to her expression when it was not relieved by her habitual yet undiscriminating smile. The orange hair, heightened in colour, Blanche could see, from its original dark brown, was fashionably disarrayed, so as to give an impression of carelessness, to which the girl added by running her fingers through it, lifting it almost amorously from the nape of her neck. Her strange black cotton clothes hinted at the unfettered body beneath, and made anything more conventional look both stingy and costive. A free-running emotion was mirrored in her appearance, as if she were only to be glimpsed in passing, as she sauntered on some mysterious progress, her motives known only to herself. She had, Blanche thought, a legendary look. Beside her, the child was almost inconspicuous, and in her cheap bright colours, so out of tune with the evident seriousness of her character, pathetic.

A nurse, coming out through double glass doors, to see if there were anybody left, checked an exclamation as she saw the girl.

'Mrs Beamish! The doctor can't possibly see you now! You were nearly an hour late for your appointment. You'll just have to come back next week.'

All the lines in Mrs Beamish's face were drawn down suddenly, revealing sharp furrows in her slightly lifted upper lip. She was evidently used to this kind of reproach.

'What does it matter?' she said, with a hint of haughtiness. 'I'm always kept waiting when I get here. I think you pack us all in here for the doctor's convenience anyway. And if he's still here I don't see why he can't see us now. I'm sure you don't want me to come back next week. And I'm quite sure I don't want to, so that makes two of us.'

'Not only can he not see you, but you can't even make another appointment,' said the nurse, bristling not so much at the girl's insolence as at her appearance. 'The receptionist's gone off duty.'

'What about this lady?' said the girl, indicating Blanche.

'Mrs Vernon is a volunteer,' said the nurse, scandalized. 'And she's usually on the wards; nothing to do with this section. No, the best thing I can do is suggest that you come back tomorrow and make another appointment. The doctor's just leaving,' she added firmly, seeing the girl rise to her feet with a sudden lifting of the drooped features as the double doors opened once more.

Blanche could hear laughter and expostulations before the little group – the woman, her child and the subjugated doctor – disappeared back through the double doors. She was left to hear the nurse's grievances as she lingered, and, unwilling to leave, encouraged her to comment on Mrs Beamish's character, although it was the child who concerned her. She learned that Mrs Beamish and her daughter put in infrequent and irregular appearances, always with demands that something should be done quickly, although long and patient investigations would have to be undertaken if any kind of reasonable diagnosis were to be arrived at. The little girl had never spoken, but, as she was not deaf, and was apparently in good health, the trouble was obviously psychic; the nurse, her lips pinched, seemed to think the fault lay in a lack of mothering. Chafed by her stiff belt and her heavy shoes, the nurse implied that Mrs Beamish's fashionable light-heartedness was somehow disreputable, as if anyone as thin as that could not possibly be adequate as a parent. Or even as a substitute parent.

'It can't have been easy for her,' ventured Blanche.

'I'll give you that. And with the husband away all the time. But I mustn't go on. You'll be wanting to go home, Mrs Vernon. And I expect you'd like to go back on the wards next week, wouldn't you?'

'Oh, no,' said Blanche. 'I much prefer it here.' She found herself watching the double doors, until it was clear that Mrs Beamish had succeeded in seeing the doctor and would not be available for a very long time.

Blanche's motives were perfectly clear to her, as she made her careful way through the side door; she was always quite conscious of her aberrations, which was why they rarely got out of hand. She was possessed by a sudden desire to know more about this woman and her child, and the initial intimation of love she had felt for the little girl eating her cake was now broadened and flattened into a need for information, for confidences, for a means of exchange. If she thought, with an old half-mocking cynicism, that she might be able to help them, she knew, beyond a doubt, that they would provide a focus of interest for her, and that if she mourned the family she had never had, she might just as well make use of these feelings in as sensible and as mutually beneficial a way as possible. Blanche was not an hysterical woman and she saw no unbecoming infatuation developing from her curiosity. Sympathy, she thought; sympathy and interest: surely I cannot be indicted for those?

Blanche did not deceive herself: she knew that her perceptions were awry. She knew that she, a stranger, could not hope for intimacy with a woman so young and so evidently self-sufficient. She also knew that she did not desire intimacy with such a woman, having registered that unusual sight of otherness, that resemblance to the invulnerable and patrician nymphs of the National Gallery's Italian Rooms. What drew her to the couple was not the simple longing of a middle-aged woman for a child. There was nothing of the predator in Blanche. What she felt was, to an extent which almost alarmed her, disinterested. She wanted merely to observe the child, to study her, to make her laugh. She would do this in the humblest possible capacity, in the light of such natural impulses as might be appropriate in the circumstances, however they might present themselves. She could think of nothing more extended than this sort of acquaintanceship, the only kind that she allowed herself these days. And yet she felt a powerful stirring of curiosity, a call from the outside world to involve herself, despite the incongruity of the encounter. She felt as if some mild signal had been given, to which she had in some mysterious and unstated way replied.

Since living alone she had experienced varying degrees of exclusion, and, out of sheer dandyism, had made an ironical survey of the subject. The dinner partner so far gone in age or indifference as to shed a bleak light on her hostess's intentions; the withdrawal, at awkward times of the year, such as Christmas, into the fortress of the family, thus precluding the proffering of invitations; the stories of rapturous holidays, to which she merely opposed her amused and attentive gaze; and those friends of other days – and they were always busy – who would say to her, 'But I mustn't go on about myself. What have *you* been doing with yourself? Anything nice?', this remark being prefaced with a look of deep commiseration. She had found no answer to the hungry curiosity of such friends, but remembering her mother's maxim – 'The best revenge is living well' – had merely continued to dress, to leave her home, to pay her cultural visits, as if invulnerability and enlightenment were to be her portion, as if to expect or to hunger for anything else were quite simply beneath her dignity. Thus she irritated many people, particularly those who were anxious to pity her. Blanche refused to be pitied. But at night, after two or three glasses of wine, she would feel her defences fall away, and her mood, heightened artificially by the anticipation of Bertie's visit, would dissipate as soon as it became clear that he would not come. At such times, standing motionless in her dusky room, or pulling aside the curtain on to the dark and empty garden, she would know an inner desolation that no one must be allowed to suspect. This desolation, compounded with the relief that somehow the day had ended, would accompany her to her bed, where, the wine having fulfilled its purpose, she would usually sleep soundly. But when she did dream she would be aware, whatever the dream's context, of the shadow of an accompanying smile, a smile that contained both mockery and mystery, the smile of the Goddess with the Pomegranate that had once so alarmed her and had left so strong an after-image that it seemed to steal up on her in unguarded moments, even in sleep.

Therefore she asked nothing from the child or from the child's mother. She merely thought it sad that they should have to visit the hospital; she thought too that it would be a fine thing to bring a smile to their faces, a smile of recognition, a smile of mutuality. Nothing would be asked in return, for she felt, if anything, a slight distaste for the confidences of strangers, having received so many in the course of her unaccompanied days. But perhaps a simple interest in their situation would not come amiss, placed as she was in the unintimidating position of vague benevolence conferred on her by her duties at the hospital. It was little enough, she thought, although in fact she was too frail, beneath her armour, to withstand the weight of old acquaintances, with their exaggerations of concern, and it would be of interest to her, and perhaps of some benefit, to observe so young and spirited a woman and to try to understand her connection with the little girl who did not speak, but whose manners, Blanche had noted with something like sorrow, were as punctilious as her own.

For the child in Blanche had recognized the loneliness of the little girl in the Outpatients' Department, had recognized too that her inability to speak was not organic but deliberate, that she refused, out of some terrible strength, to come to terms with the world which she perceived as abnormal, unsatisfactory, deficient. The steadiness of the child, as opposed to the effortlessness, the weightlessness, of the mother, indicated a desire for an ordered structured universe, with a full complement of the fixed points of an ordinary, even a conventional childhood. Blanche saw, with what seemed to her to be a true insight, that she was a child who would respond to regular meals, sensible food, traditional games, and a respectable, even a self-effacing mother. She saw, because she knew these things in herself, a resistance to the tired and tasteless cake, of which her mother had offered her not one slice but two; she saw also, in the child's determined manoeuvres with the teaspoon, her decision to behave well and in as sophisticated a manner as possible, not allowing the disappointments of life with so incompatible a parent to break down her dignity, and even assuming a little more dignity than was customary in the face of such disappointments.

All of this Blanche thought about intently, but without perplexity. For a recognition on two levels had come about: recognition of the mother as the embodiment of that essence that had seemed to mock her, offering its wordless smiling comment on her empty afternoons, and recognition of the child as being one like herself, refusing, at a heroic level, the role that was offered her and which she considered unsuited to her desires. What those desires might be Blanche did not know, could not see. But she perceived the heroism in the stance, and she required, almost painfully, to see it at close quarters, and to dismantle it, if possible, before it was too late.

And it had been said that the father was away all the time. Blanche immediately assumed him to be in prison. Was this, then, a form of hunger strike, a waiting, such as she knew from her own experience, for some impossible return? In that case, why was the mother, Mrs Beamish, so light-hearted? And so well-dressed? If there were something like prison in the background there might be money difficulties, for surely the little girl's impediment could be better served by private treatment rather than haphazard visits to a crowded hospital department. And if there were money difficulties Blanche could see a way in which she might be of help. Her status as an almost wealthy woman, a woman, moreover, who spent very little on herself but would be very happy to spend her money on someone else, would make that entirely possible.

The more she contemplated her life as it was, the more hopeless she found it to be. A sterile round of almost unmotivated activities, the evenings long and drawn out with waiting, the silent vigils by darkened windows that preceded her nights, were not enough to sustain a life, however gallant and determined. And her odd demeanour, she knew, had worn out everybody's efforts at comprehension, for she was aware that she was seen as obstinate, unassimilable, refusing to join groups of people like herself for purposes of travel or instruction, in which activities she might be supposed to involve herself honourably, thus leaving the world with no obligations towards her. Blanche knew that there was a limit – very soon reached, in her case – to the efforts one can make on one's own. It is the sign from outside oneself that delivers such beleaguered lives, lives immersed in the quicksand of their own dolorous reflections, and for some mysterious or even superstitious reason she saw her encounter with Elinor and her mother as embodying that sort of sign. Why this should be she did not know. It was simply that on this particular afternoon at the hospital she had sensed an intensification of her usually abstracted energies, had begun to think of the child, and now indeed of the mother, with something like a creator's imagination. Her business with them was not over, she thought. In fact it was just about to begin.

The evening was overcast, with a grey blanket of cloud that would simply darken imperceptibly, bringing with it the inevitable rain. There was no point in hurrying home, for home was untenanted and unattractive, therefore no longer home. Bertie would certainly not look in this evening after his visit yesterday: he liked to retain the option of staying away for unpredictable lengths of time, not wishing to witness too frequently Blanche's immaculate recitation of *non sequiturs.* In the intervals between his visits Blanche thought with envy of his fearless involvement with the messier side of life, and even of his labours in Mousie's chaotic kitchen, feeling herself too monumental ever to commit an untidiness. She practised a scrupulous avoidance of any reference that might be construed as malice or unkindness. When Bertie had told her that he was leaving her for Mousie, she had merely said, 'Yes, I rather gathered that you might be,' with a ghastly smile, the blood draining from her cheeks. She now thought that she had been spiritless and disappointing. But she was aware that Mousie, whom she knew to be a type of emotional gangster, given to hijackings and other acts of terrorism, was in fact uncomfortable with her own particular style of endurance, and feared an outbreak of lawlessness for which she must be on her guard. Bertie's visits were licensed, Blanche thought, so that Mousie could be prepared if necessary to counter any opposition that might be forthcoming; Mousie, and in her train, Bertie, could not quite give Blanche credit for her unnerving good behaviour, which they saw as having a natural term. They preferred to meet the day of her inevitable revolt with a united front. But Blanche hoped that Bertie might have his own private thoughts about her: hoped, though had no way of knowing.

She turned in to a supermarket to buy a bottle of wine and encountered her virtuous neighbour, Mrs Duff, whose anxious hand on Blanche's arm belied her reassuring smile and whose overtures of friendship Blanche had so far resisted, sensing in the woman a need to sympathize which might prove too much for her own comfort. Alone of all her acquaintances, Blanche thought, this woman treated her as if she might be wounded, and perversely she felt irritated rather than grateful. Blanche found it intolerable to have witnesses at her defeats; therefore she gave no sign of being defeated. Or so she hoped.

'A little warmer at last,' offered Mrs Duff. 'We shall soon

50

be out in the garden again.' For they shared adjoining gardens behind their respective mansion flats, and although Blanche never sat there she sometimes looked down from her window at Mrs Duff, taking the afternoon air, in a print blouse and a dazzling white skirt, on high summer days.

They made a little conversation about the weather, what it had been like, what it seemed to be about to be like, what was promised for the days ahead, in tones of great cordiality, as such acquaintances will. Blanche felt a pang of regret that she was not able to respond to Mrs Duff's overtures in a spirit of open-mindedness or the sort of mutual congratulation that would bring a smile to Mrs Duff's face. Her enormous consciousness of her own defeat had removed her, apparently for ever, from such an exchange of compliments. There was an innocence about Mrs Duff that Blanche rejected, as no longer hers to share. It was as if she herself had lost her own innocence, could think only in tortured worldly terms, must apply her censorship to every action, every word, and was oddly fearful of revealing herself to others. Yet despite all this, the little girl, perhaps because of her wordlessness, had struck some response from Blanche, had penetrated her defences, and, perhaps for that very reason, was seen to be significant.

Blanche watched Mrs Duff's figure marching trimly in the direction of home and, after a short delay, followed her out into the street. The damp evening closed round her, numbing her responses. Looking up, she saw at the bus stop on the other side of the road Mrs Beamish and Elinor, who had evidently managed an appointment with the doctor after all. Instinctively, she raised her hand and waved. Mrs Beamish nodded and smiled, then patted her daughter on the shoulder and indicated Blanche. After a second's thought Elinor lifted up her arm and waved back.

'Yes,' said Blanche later on the telephone to Barbara. 'Quite an interesting day. Not bad at all.'

F O U R

At the last moment, as she was about to leave her apartment, Blanche heard the telephone. When she learned that Barbara had succumbed to influenza, she put down her bag, walked to the kitchen and began to assemble supplies, planning in her mind the asparagus soup, the braised wing of chicken, the casserole for Jack's dinner that would occupy her for the rest of the day. Like a soldier at the barricades, she maintained herself in a state of grim good health, ever fearful of the hazards of falling ill. She had therefore survived the mild 'flu epidemic that had claimed her sister-in-law and seemed to herald the untimely arrival of summer; it had arrived with the warm but still wet weather that now dripped morbidly from the leaves of chestnut trees and greeted every morning with a spectacular show of vapour, the impotent sun a hazy white smudge in an otherwise colourless sky. The delicate steam of her soup, scenting the kitchen, made her think of greenhouses, of wet grass, and of the sun breaking through to shine on rain-spotted windows. Sweating the onion for her casserole and chopping the leek and the carrot, she reflected how glad she was to have an opportunity of doing some substantial cooking again, having restricted herself to stark single items of nourishment for far too long; her attitude to her own well-being was largely functional, without indulgence, easily despatched.

'And yet I manage to keep quite well,' she said to

Barbara, later that morning. 'There is no need to worry about me as you do. Worry about yourself instead. And drink a little more of this coffee. It is so good for you, whatever they say. Such a heavenly smell. It will soothe your poor head, and make it think of better days.'

'I can't smell a thing,' said Barbara. 'Take it away. But you are very kind, Blanche. I had forgotten what a kind woman you were. I suppose it is because you don't pretend to be kind, as so many people do. Have you noticed? It is difficult to know how to deal with such people, the sort who say, "If I had known you were ill I should have done something." And yet you would never let them know because it would be tactless, a sort of intrusion. You would not assume them to be available.'

'Perhaps you should never assume that people are available,' said Blanche, removing cups and plumping up pillows. 'Why should they be? But you are right about kindness. Genuine kindness is actually rather rare, more rare than one would imagine. I think it ought to be a cardinal virtue, and yet you don't see too much of it. Not in the past, certainly not in painting. I have been thinking about this a lot. You know I go to the National Gallery quite a bit?'

'Too much,' said Barbara, blowing her nose. 'Nobody needs to go that much. It is becoming an obsession with you.'

'Well, but you see, I am trying to decipher all those expressions. They are held up to one as standards of excellence, to be always admired, and yet there are many terrible lessons there. One realizes that even the Holy Family didn't have a lot of time for the rest of creation. We will not even speak of the Crucifixion, if you don't mind. And all the martyrdoms. Those poor saints, throwing away their lives, the only possession they could really call their own. And the cruelty of their tortures. All so that they could be shown in painting, resurrected, in perfect form, with merely a tower

53

or a key or a wheel as a dainty allusion to their sufferings. As if the realm of painting were taking its lead from the kingdom of heaven. I worry about that a lot.'

'Well, then, don't look at these things if they upset you.'

'There is actually worse to come, if you turn to the pagans. They recline on clouds absolutely impervious to everything and everyone. No kindness there. No begging for mercy from the ancient gods – they would laugh. They obey a different code, and it is exceedingly difficult to know what it is. It fascinates me. You are wrong to say that I shouldn't study these things. It is quite harmless, and it is very instructive. I am learning a lot. Only it is rather difficult at the moment to work out exactly what I am learning. That is why I keep going back.'

'Will you go there today? You don't have to stay here, you know. I shall probably sleep this afternoon, now that I don't have to worry about Jack's dinner.'

'I'll look in this evening and put it in the oven for him. And you can have a little soup then, if you want to sleep now.'

'Don't go to the National Gallery, Blanche,' said Barbara. 'It is bad for you to wander about on your own like this. Isn't there something you could . . .'

'Why, no,' said Blanche, in some surprise. 'There is nothing sinister about my visits. I am not deranged, you know. And I have always wandered about on my own, even when I was married.' She laughed. 'Don't worry about me. I'll look in this evening. Take care.' She bent to kiss Barbara, then left the house, closing the door quietly behind her.

The street was blessedly normal, after the rigours of the sickroom. Gratefully, she breathed in the mild damp air. Across the street she saw Mrs Beamish and her child at the bus stop and instead of contenting herself with a wave, she went over to speak to them. The child, Elinor, was today wearing yellow, which assorted ill both with her serious

54

face and with the jaundiced weather. She looked pale and disengaged, but gave the impression that she was furiously thinking. Mrs Beamish, although dressed in a spiralling garment of grey cotton, which, Blanche noted, was expensive and fashionably Japanese, looked paler and even more discontented than the child, her pointed features drooping, her expression withdrawn.

'Hello, Elinor,' said Blanche. 'How are you today?'

'She's a very naughty girl, aren't you?' said the mother, giving the child's hand a shake. 'She wouldn't stay with the child-minder. After all the trouble I went to to find her one. And now I've got to drag her up to town with me. And I did want an afternoon on my own for once.'

'She certainly won't enjoy it in this weather,' murmured Blanche, looking down at the face so studiously devoid of expression. 'Perhaps if you waited until tomorrow...'

'I can't wait,' the girl burst out. 'I'm going to meet an old friend, and he was going to give me lunch, and now it's all ruined.'

Yes, Blanche thought, it is ruined. The child wanted to prevent you from meeting this old friend because she is defending her father's position. And again she marvelled at Elinor's strength.

'If you like,' she said carefully, 'she could come home with me while you have your lunch. I could give her something to eat and you could collect her later. Would you like that?' she asked, bending down to Elinor. In reply Elinor put her hand into Blanche's outstretched hand and nodded. She has made her point, Blanche thought, and now she is hungry. What could be more natural? She knows she must survive.

'Well, if you're sure,' said Mrs Beamish, with no hesitation, her features instantly swept up into a dazzling smile. 'Look, Nellie, go with this lady and I'll come and get you this afternoon. There's a taxi. Quickly. Oh, terrific.'

'I live just across the road, that building on the corner,'

Blanche called after her. 'Do you see? The bell is marked Hubert Vernon.'

'Hubert Vernon,' echoed Mrs Beamish, out of the window of the taxi. 'Be a good girl, Nellie. I'll come for you later.'

Hand in hand, Blanche and Elinor walked away from the bus stop, Elinor leading the way, Blanche smiling to left and right, smiling at Mrs Duff, at the greengrocer, at the postman. She relinquished the prospect of the National Gallery without reluctance, enjoying the feel of the little girl's hand tugging at her own. The child seemed quite composed, not at all discountenanced by this turn of events, and determined to take advantage of any arrangements that were likely to forward her own inscrutable plan to grow up as quickly as possible. She seemed to sense in Blanche a certain reliability, not only in the form of her lunch but as far as the rest of the day's programme was concerned, although Blanche had no idea what that might be. A weak sun emerged; pavements dried, giving off a smell of concentrated damp. Blanche bought a small brown loaf and a pound of apricots.

'Well, I never,' said Miss Elphinstone, resting a pink rubber-gloved hand on the jamb of the kitchen door. 'Who's this, then?'

'Her mother is a friend from the hospital,' said Blanche, putting the apricots to stew in a little brown sugar. 'I said I'd give her lunch,' she added, in the tone of one granting an unimportant favour.

'Well, now, my lovely, let's have a look at you,' said Miss Elphinstone, taking off her gloves and unbuttoning Elinor's yellow waterproof. 'What's your name, then?' Elinor stared gravely into her face and made no answer. 'Cat got your tongue, has he? You come and sit down nicely and talk to me, then. What were you thinking of giving her by way of lunch?' she asked Blanche.

'I thought, scrambled egg and brown bread and butter, and these stewed apricots. By the way, don't be surprised if she doesn't answer. She doesn't speak,' she mouthed, over Elinor's head.

'Oh, maladjusted, is she?' replied Miss Elphinstone in her normal tone of voice. 'Obstinate, more like. You'll mind your manners in this house, miss,' she added, but when Blanche's back was turned her long dry hand reached out and stroked the child's cheek.

Seated at the table, they both watched Elinor intently, as she ate her lunch with slow but careful movements. Several times Miss Elphinstone reached out and cut up the child's bread and butter into unnecessarily small pieces. 'My word, she's a deep one,' she remarked to Blanche, accepting another cup of coffee. 'Seems to have taken to you, though.' The kitchen, warmed by this unaccustomed activity, presented an uncharacteristic air of disorder. 'I'll just give you a hand with these dishes,' said Miss Elphinstone, reluctant to leave. 'I expect you'll want to put her down for an hour.'

When Blanche returned from the bedroom, it was to find Miss Elphinstone packing her gloves away in her bag and very slowly adjusting her hat in the glass. 'I could give you a hand with her, if you like,' she remarked. 'I'm not wanted at church until six o'clock. And there'll be trouble there this evening or my name's not Sylvia Elphinstone.' Normality required a certain amount of discussion on this matter, so that it was three o'clock before Miss Elphinstone decided to commit herself to the bus that would take her to Fulham, where her basement flat was situated one street away from Bertie's up and coming semi.

A child-minder, thought Blanche, moving soundlessly about the bedroom while Elinor, flushed, slept in Blanche's own bed. And what sort of a woman would entrust her child to a comparative stranger? She is not to know that I am famously above board. And the father away. And the mother going out to meet a friend, reluctant to take Elinor with her. Secret lives, she thought, determined to learn more. She telephoned the hospital, obtained Mrs Beamish's address, which was down by the river, quite near, in fact, and decided to take Elinor home, not wishing, for a reason she preferred to leave obscure, to admit Mrs Beamish into her own flat, and in any event thinking that she would not remember the address, which she had repeated mindlessly in her anxiety to get away to her rendezvous.

Elinor awoke beautifully from her sleep, drank a glass of milk, and had her hands and face washed. Then they set out on their walk, in the damp but bright afternoon, for it was to have the child's hand in hers and to see the smiles on the faces of passers-by that Blanche desired, and her desire was almost equal to her curiosity. In the newsagent's she bought a book about animated trains, which Elinor carried in her free hand. And at four-thirty they descended a set of area steps to what Blanche instantly thought of as Mrs Beamish's grotto, having it by now firmly fixed in her mind that Elinor's putative mother was in fact a sort of nymph and thereby related to those persons whose mythological smiles she had questioned so endlessly on those afternoons so different from this one, afternoons which usually ended in a downcast return to her own lumpen status, vainly seeking transcendence, or at least translation, in whatever wine happened to be available that evening.

But the grotto, to which she was admitted, it seemed to her, after some interval and only after a telephone receiver was at last put down, was dusty, and flies circled above the sugar bowl when the tea-trolley was eventually organized. An imperviousness to contingencies was apparent in the mixture of style and squalor which were the most evident characteristics of the room. Mrs Beamish half sat and half lay on a lumpy brown Victorian *chaise-longue*, covered in a coarse material which showed signs of a cat's scratches, the wood of its elaborately fretted frame harbouring stray secretions of fluff. An afghan, crocheted in alternate squares of purple and cream, was thrown carelessly over one end of it, the end at which a leg trembled on its castor every time Mrs Beamish made a move. Splendid orange velvet curtains, newish in appearance, were pulled imperfectly back to reveal tall windows spattered with the dried spore of old raindrops. An equally splendid dark green carpet had obviously been amateurishly or hastily laid since it rose up in eddies around the legs of chairs and shrank from the corners of the room, revealing glimpses of bare wooden boards. The *chaise-longue* was complemented by a large squarish sofa with a row of cushions propped up against its back; this was draped in the same brownish cloth as the *chaise-longue*, with an equally fatigued appearance, although the cushions were covered in an expensive flame-coloured Thai silk. A low curving brown velvet chair on a wooden frame, with wooden arms and legs, in a Fiftyish design, occupied the space opposite an empty green-tiled hearth, even more dusty, with a pottery jar of honesty in the space where the fire should have been lit, for the room smelt musty and was probably damp. Blanche sat on an opulent square leather *pouffe*, part of an ambitious reclining chair, the major part of which had disappeared. Elinor sat on her own small chair, in exploding basket weave, reading her book.

This was Mrs Beamish's domain, for it was clear that at night she occupied the sofa with the flame-coloured cushions, lying across its considerable expanse in a long flimsy dressed-up garment and watching for passers-by through the barred windows with their careless and random accumulations of orange curtain. Where Elinor slept was not immediately apparent. Though imperfect, the room might have been designed to receive visitors: whether reclining on her *chaise-longue* or her sofa, Mrs Beamish would have the air of expecting messengers, tributes. She was both queenly and accessible, and someone, somewhere, in the background had had resources, for the cups, though marked by hairline cracks, were of fine china and had been riveted, their deep curving saucers of a nineteenth-century pattern. On a wavering trolley, the teapot was a flattened silver oval, of modern Danish design, as were the teaspoons. The remains of a chocolate cake lay on a creased bag on a glass cake dish such as might have come from Woolworth's before the war. The milk was in a bottle.

Mrs Beamish's perfect appearance – orange haired, her eyelids half closed over slanting eyes, her small brown foot emerging from the intricate tube of lavender grey cotton that was her dress – belied the hasty assemblage of the room and made it seem a temporary background to which she was very properly indifferent. It was clear that she had assumed her maternal role in the same temporary spirit, for there was no evidence of a child's games or pastimes, although the room was untidy enough to accommodate both. But Mrs Beamish's mythological status would give her a careless attitude towards children; nymphs are not known for their maternal feelings, although they lend themselves, for brief periods, to the business of nurture. The absent husband, who must certainly, Blanche thought, be in prison, had clearly not married this girl out of a desire to provide a second mother for his child, although he may vaguely have wished that it might be so; he had married her for her long slender body and her discontented brooding face, her disabused eyelids. Yet whatever her disappointments, she had an air of passing lightly through life, of passing on, and leaving little trace. She could be, Blanche thought, and probably was, formidable.

'Have you lived here long?' Blanche enquired, her cooling transparent tea revealing a previous stain in the cup.

'About a year. The lease was up on our old place and we had to find something quickly before my husband went

60

abroad. We'd never have considered this place otherwise. Nowhere for Nellie to play and horribly damp. But a friend of ours, a painter, was going to the States for a year and he let us have it for nothing. So we couldn't refuse.'

Yes, thought Blanche, admitting the plausibility of this story. It would be a painter. It is always painters who live in such squalor, considering their thoughts to be on a higher plane. On Art, in fact. But art is about aristocracy and subversion, a deeper subversion than this. And out of the corner of her eye she saw the archaic smile again, and felt it hang in the air for a moment, before it disappeared.

'And your husband,' she said, with some trepidation. 'Will he be away for long? I expect he misses the little girl.'

'Oh, Paul,' replied the girl, with a disgusted laugh. 'He works for an American, a beast, I hate him. He's horribly rich and he has houses all over the place; and he's frightfully difficult and impatient and that's why he needs Paul. He uses him like a bloody factotum, if you'll pardon my French. That's where they are now, France. I don't know where, exactly. Buying another house, I daresay.'

'But if he's American, why can't he do this for himself?' asked Blanche, bewildered by the idea of a primitive millionaire with an exquisite sophisticate in his entourage, like an eighteenth-century dancing master, employed to teach deportment.

'Because he's some sort of weirdo who's struck it rich and needs my husband's knowhow and languages. Paul's clever; he could live anywhere. We lived abroad when we were first married; we met this American in Paris and he hired Paul straight away. Then Paul insisted that I come home and look after the baby, although as far as I could see she was much better off with his mother. I need never have come into it, as far as she's concerned. Funny little thing,' she added indifferently.

'It all sounds very unusual,' said Blanche, her curiosity

61

magnificently compensated. 'I hope this American pays your husband well. You both deserve a better place than this.'

'Who, Demuth? Don't make me laugh. He made Paul sign a contract – I was dead against it – so that if he stays with him he gets a huge lump sum at the end of the year, paid into various accounts. In the meantime, he lives as family. Very well, too. Very addicted to high living is my Paul.'

'But in the meantime,' said Blanche thoughtfully, 'you have to live like this? Of course, it's only temporary,' she added, seeing a slight hauteur enter the girl's expression. 'But, as you say, there's nowhere for Elinor to play.'

'Yes, it's crappy. But, like I said, it's free, and by the end of the year we should be well off. Which is just as well because just now,' she laughed, 'it's a little difficult. Neither of us has ever been poor, you see. All our stuff had to go into store. So I keep having to buy new. Nellie needs clothes all the time, of course. Fortunately I was able to bring some of my own from Paris, and Paul is supposed to be sending the rest. But as you say, or maybe you didn't, maybe I'm just going by the expression on your face, it's lousy here. I'm not leaving my red fox coat to moulder away down here, thank you very much. I'm letting Mrs Demuth store it for me in her wardrobe, free of charge. And a few other things.' She laughed.

'How perfectly fascinating,' said Blanche.

'You thought Paul was in jug, didn't you?' said the girl shrewdly. 'Most people do. Well, he isn't.' She lit a cigarette and stared out of the window. 'Raining again,' she added.

'If I can help you with Elinor,' murmured Blanche tentatively, not wishing to give offence.

'Well, thanks. I'll remember. Mrs Hubert Vernon. What does your husband do?'

'Whatever he does is nothing to do with me any more,' said Blanche with an unhappy laugh. 'We're divorced. I

have a little money of my own.' And then wished that she
had not said that. But why not? she thought. I have been
cautious for far too long. And I did want to know. And
now I do. And must probably be prepared to pay for
my entertainment. The thought did not please her but she
managed to suppress it for the time being.

Moving between her inner and outer worlds as she did –
as she supposed most people did – Blanche was forced to
the conclusion that her previous life had been deficient in
every way. Timidly trying to confront reality, she had
misjudged the density of reality itself. Waiting, always waiting, for something to happen, she was constantly surprised
when it did. And when confronted with the reality of other
lives, she felt herself to be unprepared, and therefore all the
more desirous of understanding that reality. That she, a
respectable middle-aged woman, who, as recently as that
very morning, had enacted the age-old role of respectable
middle-aged women in succouring her ailing sister-in-law
with wings of chicken, should now, in a state of suppressed
excitement, be sitting in this artist's bower, with its smell of
musty damp and its circling flies, would have seemed to her
incomprehensible if it had been put to her in bald terms or
told to her of somebody else. She saw suddenly and precisely
something that had previously only appeared to her in a
vague and nebulous light: a great chasm dividing the whole
of womanhood. On the one side, Barbara with her bridge
evenings and her gouty husband, Mrs Duff with her girlish
respectability, and her own awkward self, and on the other
Mousie and her kind and Sally Beamish, movers and shakers,
careless and lawless, dressed in temporary and impractical
garments, and in their train men who would subvert their
families, abandon their wives and children, for their unsettling companionship. On the one side the evangelical situation – and Miss Elphinstone too came into it at this point –
and on the other the pagan world. For 'good' women,

Blanche thought, men would present their 'better' selves, saving their primitive and half-conscious energies for the others. And she herself, she further thought, had made the mistake of trying to fashion herself for the better half, assuming the uncomplaining and compliant posture of the Biblical wife when all the time the answer was to be found in the scornful and anarchic posture of the ideal mistress.

That Sally Beamish was to be found among the latter she did not doubt. For was it not Blanche who now offered to put Elinor to bed, while Sally, brooding on her day's mysterious adventures, lit another cigarette and remained staring out of the dirty window? 'Oh, she's not tired yet,' said Sally, with a vague look at Elinor, who had read her book silently and immovably throughout tea. 'The point is, what are we going to eat tonight? I didn't have time to do any shopping.' Well, you can work that one out for yourself, thought Blanche, with a return to her old asperity, although she had automatically put the cups on the trolley and wheeled it through to the kitchen, moved less by good manners than by an evil desire to know the worst.

The kitchen was indeed all that she had expected, and possibly more. Under a weak hanging light two more flies were circling over an old gate-legged table, its polish long gone, its surface grey and scarred with bleached rings. A smeared window looked out on to a small area of mossy flagstones and blackened brick, in the corner of which the falling rain gurgled through a choked pipe. The draining-board of a stone sink held a washed pile of mugs, plates, and cheap knives and forks. Since there appeared to be no cupboards, most of the kitchen's contents were piled on the table: half a loaf of bread, standing in its own field of crumbs on a bread-board, an open packet of Earl Grey tea, two jars of spaghetti sauce, two green apples, a bottle of milk, a carton of orange juice, a very expensive Le Creuset casserole, an equally expensive flowered enamel saucepan, something in a brown paper bag, some kitchen foil, and a brown earthenware teapot with a chipped spout. Removing the lid, Blanche found this to be full of cold tea and could not refrain from tipping it out and rinsing the pot. Having done this, she was led naturally into removing the washing-up from the draining-board, but on second thoughts rinsed it through again and left it, neatly stacked, where she had found it. The bread she covered with the foil, disturbing one of the flies as she did so. The cake went back into its bag. She started guiltily, as if surprised in a luckless form of trespass, as Sally Beamish and her child materialized behind her.

'She's tired, all of a sudden,' said Sally, as Elinor, inscrutable, sat high in Sally's arms with an arm round her neck. 'She wants to go to bed.'

'Did she say so?' asked Blanche eagerly.

'Oh, no, she never says anything. But we understand each other, don't we, Nellie?'

She smiled in genuine friendship at the child, whose arm tightened about her neck. For a second their heads bent together and touched. So this is how it looks, thought Blanche: parity. The parity of pagan innocence. To hide the look of longing which she was sure was printed on her face, she turned away, but, as she did so, said, 'Shall I give you a hand with her?'

I am like Miss Elphinstone, she thought, Christian behaviour masking brute hunger, the same hand stretching out of its own accord to stroke the child's cheek. But Elinor turned away, her mood having changed: now she was at one with her laughing mother and that mother not displeased, Blanche noted, to see the child's gesture of repudiation.

Heavy hearted, she followed them into the small dark room that housed Elinor's bed and her chest of drawers, on which sat a huge snowy teddy bear, a present, Blanche judged, from Paris. In the grubby gloom a nightlight was lit and placed by the bed; Sally's face was illuminated most beautifully as she bent over the flame, her expression calm and wise. She seemed in no way surprised by the way her day had turned out, or at Blanche's continued presence. In this both mother and child were alike.

They left the child, clasping an older dirtier bear and already half asleep, and went back into the living-room. Blanche felt a sudden longing for her own austere blue and grey drawing-room, a warm bath, her first glass of wine. She would wait for Bertie, although he almost certainly would not come; she even felt longing for those empty evenings of preparation and single-mindedness. Her mind was frayed, unsettled by the day's events, filled to a discordant extent with speculation. And the memory of the child's hand in hers now struck her as dangerous, something not to be cherished or brooded upon, something to be treated lightly; in fact she must treat the whole incident as lightly as Sally did herself. Involuntarily she moved to the door, intent now on her departure, her return to the life that awaited her at home.

'So if you could just tide us over,' she heard Sally say.

'Of course.' Her assent was without importance. She had no business here. She handed over five ten-pound notes and smiled vaguely at the girl's cheerful but unsurprised response.

'I'm sure Nellie would love to come and see you again,' said Sally. 'She seems to have had a lovely time. And she loves her book.'

But Blanche was now preoccupied and rather wished the girl would turn away and busy herself with her own affairs. The telephone rang. Sally made no move to answer it.

'Your telephone,' said Blanche, opening the door.

'Don't worry,' said Sally, following her. 'They can always ring back.'

The man in the restaurant, thought Blanche. The one who gave her lunch. The one she was so eager to join. And she smiled, and turned, then found herself in the area, the silent rain seeping through the moisture laden air and falling warm on her face.

Looking back from the end of the street she saw Sally, her strange corolla of a dress flattened to her body by the damp, standing at the top of the steps. She watched, as Sally looked down the road, away from her. Then she turned, and, seeing Blanche, lifted her arm in a heraldic wave. Blanche waved back. They stood there, at some distance from each other, in the rain, waving.

FIVE

Blanche dreamed that she was rowing a small boat to the Isle of Wight. The passenger in the boat was her mother, who was dressed in beige chiffon with a large straw hat. She required Blanche to row her away from the mainland because she was going out to tea and was unable to proceed under her own steam, being a decorative and frivolous woman given to iron requests which brooked no refusal. On the mainland, staring at the departing boat, was Bertie, and Blanche understood that although not wishing her to leave he was in no way disposed to prevent her from going. Blanche, in consenting to escort her mother, and thus in some way fulfilling her filial duty, was aware that she was doing a fatal thing. The proof of this was that in her hair, which was untidy, were planted four white feathers. On the further shore, to which Blanche was rowing, stood Mrs Duff, smiling and waving, applauding Blanche's act of obedience. She awoke from this dream with a beating heart and a feeling of panic.

But I did get away, she reassured herself. Although she made it so difficult for me, assuring me that a man like Bertie could not possibly be serious about a woman like me, I did get away, although Bertie himself disliked my mother and seemed at one point only too willing to concede defeat. I got away from all the duties which had been imposed on me, most of which were illusory, and all I learnt from my calculating mother was to be her opposite and not to calculate at all. Thus I began my real life in a state of awful innocence, trying to find more duties to perform, thinking myself forever indebted to the one who had sprung me from that daughterly trap, and forgetting his boredom with all forms of obedience. And aware, all the time, that my mother, who contrived a clever illness to mark my desertion, considered that she had right on her side and hogged all the attention at my wedding by feeling faint and demanding a chair at various strategic moments. Bertie ignored her, of course, but a surprising number of women, friends of hers, clustered round her and eyed me reproachfully. They seemed to have decreed for me — and for me alone — a life of forbearance, prudence, fortitude, humility: all the Christian virtues, in fact. They thought me so vague, so unpromising, that I could afford to have no desires. They often praised my goodness, by which they meant my docility, my filial servitude. Mother was almost insulted by my success. She went on a world cruise immediately afterwards, I remember, and captivated various widowers, one of whom stayed on to perform all the duties for which she had earmarked me, until her death ten years ago.

But what was Mrs Duff doing in the dream? Is it simply that she is a symbol for all the evangelical women who uphold a standard of goodness that one is not supposed to question? When I meet her in the street and refuse all her kindly invitations, is there not the same look of wistful reproach in her eyes, as if she thinks that what I really need, in my present dilemma, is her company and the company of respectable matrons like herself? As if, once fatally wounded in the war between the sexes, I should think it only appropriate to withdraw and to become modest and grateful for a quiet life? As if I must make reparation for my adventure and not sit at home by myself, drinking, or taking up with waifs and strays? She once told me, when we were both trapped at the hairdresser's, that she had met her own husband when she was sixteen, but that she had been too young to leave her mother and had made him wait for five years. And this pious although perhaps unnatural resolve is somehow all of a piece with her behaviour at the butcher's, where, unfortunately, I also meet her, and where she smartly attacks the boy for trying to sell her escalopes of veal which have already been cut and are lying palely in a dish on the block.

'Now, Brian,' she says, in a nannyish tone. 'You know my husband won't eat that.' Or, 'You know I telephoned earlier. If that fillet of beef isn't cut yet I'll send my husband to collect it later.'

For Blanche saw that Mrs Duff, secure in her married bliss, gloried in her ability to command this husband, this dentist, who had waited for her for five years, and, being a modest woman, merely demonstrated her strength in these righteous ways. And sorrowed that Blanche was unable to do the same, her eyes widening in sympathy as Blanche bought one veal chop. And was no doubt good to her mother too, and fitted both husband and mother into her contented life, having reconciled these incompatibilities without ever suspecting that they were incompatible.

Blanche, who had found her own desire to be of service almost futile, had nevertheless continued to desire to be of service, having suffered more from her original dereliction of duty than she knew. But Bertie, although accepting her efforts on his behalf, had thought them marginal, had not consciously required them, and, she knew, would have valued her much more if she had been sought after by other men, if she had been vain rather than bookish, with something of her mother's unfairness and frivolity. Thus she had come to fashion herself into an enigma, with an expression of studied indifference, which he appreciated, and which she now sought to perpetuate, all the while aware that she had failed on two counts, to be thoroughly good and thoroughly bad.

The woman that Blanche had become repudiated the Mrs Duffs of this world, seeing in them only a sanitized version of her former self, in the days when she would dreamily follow her mother, picking up her purchases, accompanying her on her numerous social engagements, longing to be free. The woman that she was then had sought to become other, and was thus attracted by all forms of disobedience, scorn, refusal, and, in addition, derision, cruelty, or the higher indifference, the true indifference to another's well being. She saw that these qualities, in some mysterious way, preserved, whereas devotion and submission, whether filial or marital, merely made one seem uninteresting. She also saw that her original misunderstandings could have been corrected by the birth of a child, who would not only be an eternal agent of reconciliation, but the recipient of her own childishness, the last hope of a good outcome in a world flawed by false expectations.

Her visits to Sally Beamish were not disinterested. She saw in the child, Elinor, the embryonic adult who could still, perhaps, after her unpromising start, be reclaimed for a life that was both sensible and rewarding. And she saw in the mother a sly comment on the investment of such energies as she possessed, saw in her the crystallization of those female qualities in which she knew herself to be deficient. A whole education seemed to await Blanche in that dusty and unattractive room, in which, perversely, she found attractions that were missing at home. And this education promised her the advancement of her own unfinished story, of her disappointed hopes, and of her unused and unrequited faculties. She would have liked to do something decisive, to temper the child's terrible fortitude, her dumb refusal of frivolous alternatives to the real meaning of life; she would have liked, in all modesty, to have proved a good friend, although whom this would benefit most was a little hazy in her mind; for she found herself to be unusually curious about all aspects of this story. It was as if, once again, she was an eager pupil in the business of living life as she supposed it should be lived, never having had real knowledge of anything except the contents of her own mind. These were the various calls that she answered as she found herself on the way to Sally's basement, promising herself that she was only 'looking in', since she had not seen Sally at the hospital since their first encounter there.

On the evenings of such days Bertie would find her distracted, flushed, quite obviously not expecting him, and, assuming that she had a lover, would become amused and rather more attentive. Blanche, recalling herself to herself, would tell him that there was a bottle of Muscadet in the fridge, and leave him to get it while she briefly regarded herself in the glass and regretted, mildly, that he had found her before she had had time to have her bath and change.

'You're looking well,' he said, on one of these evenings, appreciating anew her fine head and her distant expression. 'Going out much?'

'Yes,' she answered without guile. 'I have made a new friend.'

'Mousie would like it very much if you would come to dinner one evening. As you know, we are going away soon and I shan't see you for some time.'

'Oh, I don't think so,' said Blanche. 'I am not sophisticated enough to be able to tolerate such a civilized arrangement. I might make an injudicious remark or start raving on about Henry James.'

'I think we have heard of Henry James, you know, although of course I rely on your good taste not to embarrass Mousie.'

'You would be very unwise to count on my good taste,' said Blanche. 'I am trying to get rid of it. I plan to become dangerous and subversive. Do not look to me to be Millie Theale. A silly girl, I always thought. She should have bought that rotter outright. What else is money for?'

'And whom are you planning to buy outright?' asked Bertie, feeling a renewal of interest in her.

'Oh, no one you know,' she answered truthfully.

For these days she always left a couple of ten-pound notes under the lid of the chipped teapot in Sally's lugubrious kitchen. Neither of them ever referred to this exchange.

Yet her missionary zeal, misplaced, was never more superfluous than when Elinor was absent, staying with her grandmother, Paul's mother, in well-heeled Surrey suburbia. Blanche wondered at the antagonisms or alliances that Elinor's absence or presence signified. She wondered too about Elinor's father, of whom she had seen a photograph. This showed a smiling young man with weakly romantic good looks of a kind to seduce timorous women: abundant dark hair, shining eyes beaming forth messages of boyish goodwill, and a curved, almost feminine mouth. He looked like every mother's favourite son, and despite his rather obvious beauty Blanche surmised that he was a bore. He was certainly either rather inept or very clever, for he was apparently in thrall to the mysterious Mr Demuth, the American enigma, and was forced to act as *homme de confiance*, a position which could entail certain humiliations of a domestic nature. On the other hand, if he endured his year's apprenticeship he could count on a handsome sum of money and could come home in triumph to his wife, bearing her red fox coat, and to Elinor, with perhaps more impractical toys. And then what? Would they move away, as a family, and set up home properly? Blanche doubted it. Sally was the sort of woman who demanded to be entertained, who would expect to eat most of her meals in good restaurants, and would claim handsome compensation for her year alone with the child. And in all this Elinor would no doubt be obliged to spend more and more time with her grandmother and would remain dumb for as long as her father was absent from her life, for as long as he behaved like the usurper's lover, which, Blanche thought, he must continue to do for it was his fate to succumb to, and be controlled and frustrated by, such a woman, and he would count himself lucky to be in such a hazardous position.

In some recess of her mind Blanche was aware that her friendship for Sally Beamish was not a genuine friendship but one which had been born out of her own needs. On the second and only other occasion on which she had contrived to bring Elinor home with her for lunch she had been aware of Miss Elphinstone's slightly more critical stance.

'Well, she's taken to you and no mistake,' Miss Elphinstone had said from the doorway, until invited to join them at the table. 'But you don't want to go putting yourself out for her. She's got a home of her own, hasn't she?'

'Yes,' Blanche had replied. 'But it leaves a lot to be desired. I doubt if you would approve.'

'Whether I approve or not's neither here nor there. It's where she belongs. She's not old enough to go out visiting without her mother.'

And she had looked severely at Elinor, as if Elinor were a deserter, and did not talk to her. Elinor, perhaps sensing disapproval, had pushed her baked egg aside and refused to eat her stewed apple. Although Blanche had never seen her cry she now watched the child's face darken and had judged it wise to forgo Elinor's nap and take her out to the park. Sitting forlornly on a bench, watching Elinor play with another child's tricycle, she warned herself that she was becoming foolish, that this would not do, that there was to be no form of maternity for her, even if her fantasies had once tended that way. She saw too that Elinor was no Victorian child, dedicated to preserving the harmony of her own little family, eyes upturned, hearing heavenly voices,

74

but tough, with the toughness of one who has studied the dynamics of survival and made it her business to learn the rules. On the evening of that day Blanche bathed and changed, sat in her drawing-room with a bottle of wine, and reflected that she had caught herself just in time: she had been about to make a fool of herself again. Now she would simply do what a reasonably effective middle-class woman could do for Sally and her child and then leave them alone. But the image of what her restored independence would be failed to charm her, and she felt herself again to be a prisoner of her own fate, unresigned, yet powerless in the face of what others had decreed for her.

Blanche was not a foolish woman, although she eagerly contemplated foolishness in others, hoping to steal some lightness of touch from their behaviour. Her charitable actions towards Sally, the contributions placed under the lid of the teapot, she rightly counted as nugatory, for her motives were impure. And so it was with a wistfulness sharpened by self-criticism that she next encountered Sally Beamish's down-drooping and abstracted hospitality, and she determined to put this odd acquaintanceship on a more realistic basis, assuming once again her quizzical stance and denying for herself any part in the fortunes of these people.

This, though, was not too easy. Sally had come to rely on her in a disappointed sort of way, as if Blanche were a poor substitute – poor but available – for more active assistance. As far as Blanche could see, Sally spent those days when Elinor was absent simply lying on her *chaise-longue*, smoking, and waiting for someone to turn up. Blanche suspected that there was a man, or even men, in the background and that Elinor's removal to her grandmother's house was not unconnected with this fact. Sally had the careless smile and the genuine absentmindedness of one who was used to a constant stream of favours. Many were her references to her life before she had been marooned in this basement, but they were references to parties, holidays, tremendous sprees that did not end until the dawn of the following day, joy rides, Morocco for breakfast, dinner in Venice. Blanche assisted at these reminiscences in a subordinate capacity, wondering how Sally had had the money for this hedonistic life when she was now so obviously in need of it. The answer, as far as she could see, was with the absent Paul, who had obviously spent all he had on her, and, the money having gone, had been forced to take up this curious position with the American, Demuth.

'When is he coming home?' asked Blanche in a carefully neutral tone.

Sally shrugged. 'Your guess is as good as mine,' she said.

They were seated as usual in the basement. Blanche assumed matters to be serious, as Sally had actually telephoned and asked her to come round. Once she had done this, however, she seemed to have as little as usual to say, although she managed to indicate that Elinor would be staying with her grandmother for some time, or at least 'until we can work something out'. Her phrases habitually had a vague but modish air, explaining nothing. Blanche had done some shopping on the way, suspecting that the telephone call had been inspired by indigence, and on the pretext of putting something in the kitchen had left fifty pounds under the teapot lid. She had no way of knowing whether this was too much or too little. Judging by herself she supposed it to be enough, but then, although she was a woman of some means, she was both frugal and methodical, and all too prudent in her needs. But Sally, she could see, had higher expectations, and her original gifts of little clothes for Elinor had been met with a 'Sweet of you, but you shouldn't' and a particularly disappointed smile.

The prospect of pulling Sally into shape, which Blanche now saw as the task before her, presented some difficulties. The original animation that Sally had shown in the Outpatients Department only flashed back into life when past activities were being reviewed. The holidays, the parties, the dinners, Sally implied, were of such a superior nature that she could not be expected to put up with anything less, and it was therefore only natural that she should spend these listless though intent waking hours waiting for pleasure to be renewed. She appeared to have no ability, or no inclination, to be anything but a recipient. Her passivity seemed to mark an interval in her expectations, and in that sense to be seen by her as entirely appropriate. Where Blanche would arrive in the keen expectation of hearing definite news, or at least some plan of action, Sally, by contrast, seemed to be emptying her mind of everything apart from the memory of past activities. When these came into the conversation, as they did to an increasing extent, she would recover her lost animation; her features would sharpen, her eyes light up, and preoccupied laughter would escape her, as if the peculiar essence of these incidents could not possibly be conveyed but would be known, like a code, to those similarly advantaged. Her encompassing boredom with the present included Blanche, as Blanche could see. What was worrying was not only Sally's increasing abstraction, her removal from the dilemma of the present, as Blanche saw it, but the fact that these reminiscences seemed to be quite disparate, not anchored in real time, and above all unconnected with her husband. Sally's past life, the only one she cared to talk about, was surrounded by a crowd of people known to her only by their Christian names: who they were, what, if anything, they did, where they lived when not staying in hotels or villas – all this was outside the boundaries of her interest. It was as if they had been her companions in some mythic time when they had all moved weightlessly from party to party, resort to resort. It was a diet of hedonism, from which the fibrous content of real life had been removed.

Blanche saw, in Sally, how occasions of pleasure had bred indifference to anything less, how a continuous level of excitement had led to expectation of more, and how gratification had merely intensified her scorn for lives undistinguished by festivity. The parties of bygone days had simply prepared her for nothing but the next party: life had revealed itself as entertainment, enhancement, brilliance, and she could not see why she should do more than lend herself temporarily to her altered state. For this reason she seemed to have entered a period of hibernation, to have literally altered her body's rhythms, to have slowed down her energies to such an extent that she could spent days marooned on her *chaise-longue*, smoking, and looking thoughtfully out of the window. Her strong white teeth would occasionally crunch through a piece of toast or an apple, for, unlike Blanche, she would have thought it poor-spirited to eat a proper meal without the appropriate company and service. She continued to dress in her avant-garde garments but she had become even less communicative than before, using well-worn phrases that apparently pleased her by their handiness, and lapsing into long periods of ruminative silence.

As far as Blanche could make out, she was not ill, not depressed, not undernourished or traumatized. Rather she showed the immense lethargy of the healthy animal whose needs are not met. And Sally's basic need was apparently to live on the edge of exhaustion, over-stimulated by wine, noise, laughter, company, and the prospect of an endless rout. It became clear to Blanche that Sally's life, before her marriage, and possibly for a brief period after it, had been a sort of saturnalia, that the saturnalia had been complicated by creditors, and that the result of these complications was her exile in the basement, while her husband worked to get more money together. Blanche was both appalled and charmed by such fecklessness, and she could not but compare it favourably with her own caution, the modesty of her own expectations. She thought back, almost guiltily, to her early married life, her humble walks in the public gardens of those fashionable places, where her husband, impatient, went off to visit his friends; she thought of her visions of sunny gardens and hot days and southern markets, all known once but only in passing and long lost: how nerveless it all seemed, and how weak. She even thought, and not for the first time, that it was her timorous decency, disguised as brusqueness, that had caused her to lose Bertie, and she compared herself with the distantly musing Sally entirely to her own disadvantage. For Sally, like Mousie, like those cynical smiling nymphs in the National Gallery, had known, with an ancient knowledge, that the world respects a predator, that the world will be amused by, interested in, indulgent towards the charming libertine. At that moment Blanche knew herself to be part of the fallen creation, doomed to serve, to be faithful, to be honourable, and to be excluded. She saw that fallen creation, mournful in its righteousness, uncomforted in its desolation, and living in expectation, as she had waited long hours in her drawing-room for the hope that would not return.

Her initial sadness for the mute child was now compounded by an awful unwilling sorrow for the increasingly mute mother, and she felt that unless she resumed her resolutely composed former self she might well join them in their silence. A long and charmless vista of renewed cultural activities opened before her as she prepared to do her duty once again and to divest herself of the dubious but attractive company of Sally Beamish. For a brief moment she felt grave pain as she thought of the little girl, and even greater pain as she considered her own foolishness in wishing to – what? To adopt her? Nothing so specific. To befriend her, to contemplate her. Passive, as ever, in her loves, she had simply wanted to multiply the occasions of seeing Elinor, and was now ashamed to see her needs for what they were.

'We really must get you sorted out, Sally,' she said, finally, with a purposefulness which she did not feel. 'I imagine funds are low. What about allowances, Social Security and so on? Are you sure you are claiming all that you are entitled to?'

Sally looked at her without interest. 'I've been into all that. I'm not entitled to anything. I haven't got stamps on my card or whatever you need and I can't claim Family Allowance because Paul's working out of the country. And he hasn't got any stamps either.'

'But this is monstrous,' said Blanche. 'Do you mean there's no money coming in at all?'

'I thought you understood that,' said Sally. 'I only have what Paul's mother can send me.' For some reason neither of them mentioned the money left under the teapot. Blanche felt herself blushing and hurried on.

'And you still don't know when Paul is coming back? Have you heard from him?'

'Oh, yes, I've heard. There's some complication, apparently.' She drew her fine brows together and lit another cigarette. Her instinct, when sensing trouble, was simply to abstract herself, to empty her mind, and increase the distance from annoying topics. Now, faced with mysterious complications which were, apparently for that very reason, not to be explained, she became expressionless and remote, imposing on Blanche, by the very stillness of her body, a reticence which effectively blocked any remonstrances that might have met this remark. There was a brief silence.

'Well,' said Blanche heartily, as she put her right arm into the sleeve of her raincoat. Glancing through the smeared window she saw that a weak sun had banished the rain and that the long days were now firmly established. It would be daylight until ten o'clock. 'Is there anyone else who could help you?'

'I don't think so,' Sally replied with apparent indifference.

'As far as I can see we're on our uppers. Of course,' she added, glancing covertly at Blanche, 'Nellie will have to stay with Paul's mother until we can get things sorted out. I can't bring her back here if there's no money.'

Blanche rose to her feet. The implications of Sally's last remark were not lost on her. 'I think the best plan', she said, careful not to let her expression change, 'would be if I were to get the allowance side of things worked out. Do you know which is your local office or bureau or whatever the thing is called?' She busied herself with her empty shopping basket, rearranging things in it unnecessarily, trying to subdue the uncomfortable beating of her heart.

Sally's reaction to her *faux pas* was an increased, a heightened indifference. It was implied that all misfortunes were equally graceless and did not deserve any refinement of manners. 'Oh, don't bother,' she said. 'If you could just tide us over. My husband will straighten it all out when he comes home.'

Ah yes, thought Blanche. He is now 'my husband'. Absent, of course, but legal nevertheless. And coming home, some day.

'Let me see what I can do,' she said. 'Bertie has a friend at the Home Office. They were at Cambridge together. A nice man. I'll telephone him this evening and see if he can bring a little influence to bear.' Treat the matter as one of simple need, she thought, not of obligation, not of misplaced hope. A matter of justice, or of charity. No involvement. No more of that.

Sally's down-drooping mouth and half closed eyelids told her that her efforts would be wide of the mark. She would rather that people continued to tide her over, as she puts it, thought Blanche; probably the people in that set of hers were continually tiding each other over. That sort of person is usually characterized by prodigality and bad debts, both thought to be amusing. How cruel I have become, she thought sadly. It is as if I had never been young. I never had a bad debt in my life and now I am not proud of the fact. Perhaps a little more prodigality would have saved me. But I was careful and proud. 'The best revenge is living well.' What a fatuous remark. However, pronounced in mother's icy tones, it took on the allure of a great maxim. And this is where it has got me. Far better to be like Sally and to have misspent one's youth, even if one has to pay for it afterwards. Paying for it, however, is precisely the problem.

She emerged from the basement to a dazzle of white light, the sun beating through layers of moisture. There was an intense and sickly smell of elderflowers. This, then, was the summer, about which she had had so many inaccurate or outdated thoughts. She felt a slight tremor of panic as she contemplated the inevitable absences of those about to go on holiday: Bertie to Greece, Barbara and Jack to the cottage, even Miss Elphinstone on her coach trip. It would be her second summer alone. She bought an expensive bottle of Pinot at the wine merchants, and, feeling uninteresting and graceless in her heavy clothes, resolved to bathe and change before telephoning Patrick Fox. Having placed matters in his hands, she thought, she would, as it were, resign from the case. It seemed to her that she felt a good deal older as she contemplated this course of action.

S I X

Thinking over the events of the afternoon, Blanche wept briefly at her own foolishness, had a bath, changed, and poured herself a glass of wine, before thinking how best to tackle Patrick Fox.

On the face of it this telephone call was a simple affair. She had only to remind him of her existence, tell him that she needed his help, and suggest that he came round for a drink. Below this seamless surface, however, there were certain difficulties of a nebulous consistency. Patrick had been in love with her, to a limited extent and much to Bertie's amusement, in the days before she was married. At one point she had feared that the news of her engagement to Bertie would prove quite literally fatal to Patrick, but as it happened he had simply gone back to restoring old harpsichords, which were his true passion, and had managed to behave quite creditably when they invited him to dinner, so creditably that Blanche wondered if she had imagined the whole thing. It was difficult to tell what Patrick was feeling; that was the trouble. He had the head of a Roman legislator, with hair gone prematurely grey, and under stress of great emotion his lips would very slightly purse, which lessened his air of impregnability: otherwise, nothing changed.

'I could understand it if he would say something,' Blanche had worriedly complained to Bertie. 'As it is I don't know whether I am dealing him a mortal injury in inviting him to dinner or whether he would hate it if he were left out and simply heard about the evening from Barbara and Jack.'

'If he doesn't want to come he can always say no,' replied Bertie. 'He doesn't strike me as dying of a broken heart. Not that it would be easy to tell, of course. It surprises me that he ever had the gumption to make a pass at you.'

'Men are so crude,' said Blanche. 'How do you know he didn't see something extraordinary in me? I am not a conceited woman, as you know, Bertie. But I have certain ... qualities, perhaps, that a shy man like Patrick might have found endearing. I am a good listener. I take an interest in a man's work; well, one has to. After all, one hears so much about it. No one need be ashamed of me in public. I give away no scandalous secrets like a number of women I know. You would be surprised, Bertie, by the lewd way in which women talk to each other, their disloyalty, their cackling laughter. At the hairdresser's, even. Ready to betray their men at the drop of a hat. Egging each other on, getting out of hand. Well, no one need fear that sort of behaviour from me. What was I saying?'

'You talk too much, Blanche,' said Bertie. 'Come here.'

So she had continued to invite Patrick to dinner and had made a point of flashing him a placating smile before seating him next to the prettiest woman she could think of. He seemed unperturbed by both the smile and his partner and would eat his way judiciously through the meal and make a few equally finely judged remarks in the latter course of the evening, his long thin fingers lightly clasping his brandy glass. He would always offer to take his partner home but managed to do so with a show of good manners that only just masked reluctance. Women were offended by him. They would telephone Blanche the following morning, puzzled, unnecessarily critical, and try to find out more about him, for he was so eminently eligible that they dared not trust their instincts and let him go.

'I know nothing about him,' Blanche would say, more or less truthfully. 'He is quite high up in the Civil Service, I believe. And he loves music.' She thought that quite enough to be going on with.

'Have you got a telephone number for him? It's just that I'm giving a little party next week. I hope you'll both be free, by the way. And it might amuse him to come. I thought he seemed rather lonely.'

Yes, he is very good at giving that impression, thought Blanche, and was forced to revise her opinion of Patrick, whom she continued to think of alternately as a man of hidden fires and a cold fish. And there was that fatal evening when Bertie had suggested that it would be a kindness if she invited his new secretary, who was of course Mousie, on the pretext that she was lonely too. How did Bertie know this, Blanche had enquired. Well, he had found her weeping one day and had been obliged to comfort her. I see, said Blanche. In that case I shall invite Patrick. They can weep on each other's shoulders, tell each other what rotten childhoods they had. Not that Patrick had ever revealed such low-class information. But who knew what depths he might descend to, given the right stimulus?

Blanche remembered that evening very well. She had served a vegetable terrine, baked chicken, salad, cheese, and fresh pineapple with a raspberry sauce. Not one of her better menus, she recalled sadly, but then the whole evening had got off to a bad start when Mousie had arrived half an hour too early and had to be sent to the drawing-room with Bertie in attendance until the other guests arrived. Blanche could hear cries of, 'You know you did, Bertie. Oh, I feel awful about this. Do you suppose your wife will ever forgive me?' Miss Elphinstone, who liked to stay to set the table on these occasions, had raised her eyebrows at this; she and Blanche had exchanged a brief look, and then, 'I wonder if I should have bought another pineapple,' said Blanche. 'Two slices each would be my outside maximum,' said Miss Elphinstone firmly. 'Pineapple can lie heavy, you know.' And, slipping on her navy blue silk coat, which Blanche had bought in the Saint-Laurent sale and abandoned shortly afterwards, she had picked up her bag and said goodnight, her monastic cheeks very slightly flushed. She was an excellent woman, and, for all her propriety, she sometimes arrived at conclusions which were less than a faint suspicion in Blanche's mind. Blanche, in any event, was at that moment measuring out her rice.

That evening had given her an opportunity to see a rather clever woman at work, although Blanche missed this opportunity, as she missed so many others. She thought Mousie very boring and wondered why she kept on reverting to her mistake in arriving so early. She then wondered why Bertie had to keep on reassuring her that it did not matter, why Mousie had to clasp her hands to her cheeks, declaring that he was embarrassing her, and why even Patrick's Roman features had relapsed into a faint smile. She had merely registered the fact that Mousie had been insufficiently trained out of her attention-getting ways which had no doubt been very effective when she was younger but were surely redundant now. Teasing, of an inordinate nature, had gone on for the rest of the evening. The other guests had been Barbara and Jack, people on whom Blanche could rely to keep the party going when she was out of the room. None of it had been a success. At one point she had gone into her bedroom for a bit of peace and quiet, leaving them with their coffee; she had taken a few deep breaths of air out of her window, not knowing why she felt so tired and ill at ease. Bertie had come to find her and had reproached her, saying that her absence had unsettled Mousie, who was sure she had upset Blanche by arriving too early. 'I haven't been gone five minutes,' said Blanche wearily. 'I wasn't planning on going to bed, you know.' Although quite suddenly the

86

thought of her bed took on the splendour of a heavenly vision and she wondered how she could possibly last until all her guests had gone.

Back in the drawing-room she found Mousie, becomingly flushed, protesting that Bertie had given her too much to drink. She also found Barbara looking rather strangely at Jack, who could be heard urging Mousie to have a little more brandy. Patrick sat, his patrician features minimally relaxed, enjoying the spectacle. Mousie had not paid any attention to him throughout the dinner, and he was enjoying himself. Furthermore, he had not relished the prospect of telling her about the harpsichords, although he had been known to use them as a weapon to deflect too eager an interest in his ways. When he offered, with a show of false alacrity, to take Mousie home, Bertie had said, 'It's a bit tricky from here, a bit out of your way. Perhaps I'd better . . .' Blanche, who had lit an unaccustomed cigarette, glanced at him in surprise. Patrick, smiling fully at last, and with a certain measure of satisfaction, had kissed her goodnight and had taken Mousie by the arm. Bertie had seemed a little ruffled and tended to blame Blanche afterwards for asking Mousie how she amused herself when she was alone. 'I only meant to ask her what she did at the weekends,' said Blanche. 'It was you who told me that she was lonely. Why all this fuss? She strikes me as perfectly capable of leading her own life. And she is very pretty.' 'You may have upset her,' said Bertie gravely. 'Bertie,' said Blanche. 'I am going to bed. I strongly advise you to do the same. If she telephones me in the morning and apologizes for arriving too early I may scream.' But in the morning there was no telephone call from Mousie, and Blanche shrugged and forgot the whole thing.

All of this stood in the way of her now telephoning Patrick. And more besides. For she felt that that particular evening had marked the end of her innocence and that ever since then she had been wary, cautious, on the alert, though never sufficiently on the alert to avert surprises, usually of an unwelcome nature. And had fashioned herself into something so unimpeachably careful and scrupulous that no one would suspect the panic that had overtaken her so frequently in the months that followed. So prayerfully had she behaved, so convinced that the worst would overwhelm her, and so determined had she been to show none of this, that it was as if she had struck a bargain, and if fate proved kind and told her that she had been mistaken, then her worst suspicions need never be known and her dark imaginings left in the deepest vault of her memory that she could devise. And when the worst did happen she merely threw it off with as much amused laughter as she could muster and determined to improve herself so that nothing could afflict her again, thinking, again mistakenly, that some unworthiness in herself had brought this about, and that if she improved she would be rewarded. What that reward could now be was unclear. Before her eyes, as if to save her but also to provide her worst torment, came those sightings of Bertie in his mother's garden, or the shining seas of southern towns, or those market places where she had seen and smelt the fruit in their profligate piles. And in order to remind herself that these things still existed, that fantasies of a high order had always informed a certain reality, one to which she now had no immediate access, she had begun her visits to the National Gallery, to be met there only with the austere visions of saints, the dolorous lives of virgins and martyrs, and, most singularly, the knowing and impervious smiles of those nymphs, who, she now began to see, had more of an equivalence in ordinary life, as it is lived by certain women, then she had ever suspected.

And if I let this continue to happen, she now thought, pouring herself another glass of wine, if I were to sink into an endless fantasizing, I should be no better than Sally

Beamish, in her basement, remembering all her parties and holidays, and lapsing into a state from which others have to rescue her. Reality must be my only cure now, she thought: the art of the possible. And, as if to comment on her resolution, a passing cloud released a shower of rain.

'Patrick?' she enquired into the telephone, in a lively but neutral tone. 'It's Blanche. Blanche Vernon. Yes, it has been a long time, hasn't it? I was wondering if you could come for a drink one evening this week. Not a party,' she added hastily. 'Just me, I'm afraid. I need your advice. You couldn't possibly make it this evening, I suppose? Oh, wonderful. Half an hour?'

The telephone rang as soon as she put down the receiver.

'Blanche? Where have you been all day? I wanted to ask you to dinner this evening and now you're going to tell me it's too late. I haven't yet decided whether this is your fault or mine. You won't come, of course.'

'It's kind of you, Barbara, but I've got Patrick Fox for a drink in half an hour. You wouldn't like to join us, would you? Oh no, better not this evening: I told him I'd be alone. You know how he likes to prepare for his encounters. Another time, perhaps.'

'Patrick!' said Barbara. 'What a good idea! Yes, we must all meet again. It would be just like old times.'

'Yes,' said Blanche. 'And only Bertie missing.'

'Blanche,' began Barbara, after a slight pause. 'You don't suppose...?'

'Oh no,' said Blanche. 'I don't.' And, after a pause, she added, 'I'll ring you tomorrow and tell you how he is.'

Patrick's Roman head, she saw, was now allied to a rather pear-shaped figure. Those past few months of being an extra man at dinner had begun to take their toll. But I have probably changed too, she thought, although I can't see it myself. In fact I have changed so remarkably little that it is positively sinister. I have not gone mad and over-eaten, sobbing over the pastries, nor have I dyed my hair another colour. I have not spent any more money on clothes – much less, in fact – and my figure is still quite good. I always knew that women alone could fall into so many traps that I took good care to avoid them. Routine is important. And the frightful emptiness of the day can be overcome if one simply leaves the house at a sensible hour and does not return until one is agreeably tired. I am probably looking just as I did on that awful evening when Mousie came to dinner and which was when I last saw Patrick. But Patrick, who remembered Blanche as a handsome, reckless-looking woman, found her quite changed by the expression on her face. The eyes, which had always seemed so distant and amused, were now wide with innocence and doubt, and her movements were narrower, more hesitant. Otherwise she was recognizable, he saw thankfully, not gone to seed. By this he meant something disreputable, gipsy-like, bedraggled. He had half expected her to be trailing around in discordant garments, having read in the Sunday newspapers that the loss of a partner has a high stress count and can threaten sanity and even life; he had fully expected the door to be opened with the safety chain on, one bleared eye regarding him suspiciously through the crack. A bachelor, Patrick feared women unless they were impeccably presented and if possible exotically decked out. He put his distaste for the natural state down to his well-known love of the arts. His feelings for Blanche had been constant and severe, as if she bore a certain responsibility for causing him to think about her and even to contemplate a change in his habits. During his courtship, which was kept under such control that even Blanche wondered if she had imagined the whole thing, he behaved like a man who has just had news of a grave illness, for which he must make reluctant but decent allowance in the weeks to come. Yet he was a man of honour; at no point, contemplating the sheer inconvenience of it all, did he renounce the idea of marriage. He simply felt that it suited his dignity to treat the matter as one which would inevitably bring him some regrets, and in his efforts to hide these regrets from Blanche he was frequently reduced to saying nothing at all. Sometimes his regrets were so acute that he was forced to spend some evenings by himself, when he would wander round his large dark drawing-room, handling certain precious books, striking a poignant single note from his harpsichord and wondering if his housekeeper would leave him if he brought home a wife. One thing led to another on these evenings of abstinence, and he would tell himself that all he required after a hard day at the office was half an hour with the Meditations of Marcus Aurelius and a couple of Brandenburg Concertos: anything else would be redundant. Then he would remember Blanche's peculiar mixture of raciness and delicacy, remind himself that she had all the qualities he regarded most highly in a woman, remind himself also that his friend Bertie held the same views, and move ineluctably to the telephone to tell Blanche that he had tickets for a concert on the following evening and that he would pick her up at seven.

Blanche's guilty conscience over Patrick came not from the fact that she found Bertie a better man than Patrick but that she found him a worse one. Whereas Patrick would take her arm and guide her along pavements as though she were an invalid, Bertie, lost in thought, would frequently stride on ahead, leaving Blanche, quite happily ruminative, following at some distance behind him. Thus her fondest memories of being wooed by Bertie were simply of herself wandering, without much thought, along various streets, taking time to note how the trees were turning or which houses were being painted, and always, in blissful view somewhere ahead, Bertie, who at some point would turn round and say, 'Do come *on*, Blanche.' She supposed that she rather enjoyed this position of servility, not because it made her feel like a slave but because it allowed her to feel like a child. With Patrick one always had to dress up and have opinions on atonal music. Bertie, curiously enough, found her devoid of mystery, whereas to Patrick she was an enigma, compounded of her essential femaleness and her unexpected judgments. He appreciated her as a clever woman; Bertie very occasionally gave her an indulgent look but more often told her she talked too much.

Her mother was all for Patrick, with his finicky airs and his excellent prospects. Her mother was only too keen for her to avoid entanglements of a distressingly physical nature, which she saw as a direct insult to herself. After all, if Mrs Moore could manage so well without that kind of thing, why should her daughter not do the same? While singing Patrick's praises, which she did constantly, as a form of primitive magic or behavioural engineering, she was aware of Bertie eyeing her thoughtfully, and, it seemed to her, as if he were calculating her performance as a woman. Bertie was, she was forced to admit, appallingly straightforward. This quality, Blanche found, annihilated all others. Bertie's attitude towards her was one of simple acquisition. He saw no need to indulge in any form of mating ritual, did not tell her all about himself, did not want to know everything about her, did not create instant memories, anniversaries, landmarks in their friendship. He simply took her wherever he happened to be going himself. Blanche, hearing her friends becoming solemn and arch about their men, had often wondered whether they made things up or why they needed the reassurance of other women in order fully to enjoy them. She humbly supposed herself to be lacking in the sort of allure which she heard tell about on all sides. 'I know he finds me physically irresistible,' she heard one friend assuring another, and saw them both lift an eyebrow at each other as she came into view. On reflection she found it so much easier and more pleasant to be put in Bertie's car, driven to a site which was not always picturesque, and left on her own to moon around a farmyard while Bertie discussed his, to her, always mysterious business with someone to whom she was rarely introduced. He was the head of a firm of prosperous estate agents. Sometimes, on the way home, they would talk, but not always. She found this supremely restful. Whereas Patrick, with his enormous respect for women and his irreproachable concern for her, she found rather exhausting.

What she had not noticed, since she had no reason to believe that it extended to herself, was Bertie's great social curiosity. His interest in his work and in the world of business seemed to her so active that she supposed that he saw her simply as an area of relaxation, and she found no reason to quarrel with this. But he was always going out to dinner and when he took her with him she was quite surprised that he knew and liked so many people. Her own passivity did not seem to be an obstacle to his enjoyment but she began to become aware of it. After the early weeks of marriage, when she would run to meet him and tell him about the inconsequential activities of her day, she began to edit herself into a more worldly version of herself. And so, stealing her quiet hours away from his friends, she would prepare for them as she knew he would like her to. That was when she saw that she must pay her dues. She took a simple pleasure in pleasing him. But imperceptibly she became rather quaint and lost a good deal of her spontaneity. In this way she struck others as mildly alarming, whereas she was in fact on the lookout for his, and their, approval. This came in good measure for a time. Then, as she became less sure of herself, she sought information in books, works of fiction which would teach her a little more about society than she was able to work out for herself. Thus she knew both more and less, and sometimes had the feeling that she was ahead but more often that she was behind. Basing herself on what seemed to be unalterable authorities, she was unable to see that life had moved on, or that plans to which she had no access were being laid. She could see that Bertie was an avid social animal but not how far his animality would take him. It came as a complete surprise to her to learn that Bertie was fascinated by Mousie, because Mousie simply did not figure in her list of characters. Men who fell in love with their secretaries, even if they had the decency or the prudence to move those secretaries to another position, were, to her, characters from another kind of fiction, the kind she did not read. She supposed this secondary kind of fiction to be as powerful and as pervasive as folklore because everyone apart from herself seemed to know about it.

And, after the event, thinking that she had not learned the right lessons, she mournfully set herself to learning more. But she did not quite trust the books, which had left her unprepared, and tried a different discipline. The pictures told her another story. There were moralities here too, but of a more unsettling nature; she could see, as she now began to see in life, the discrepancy between duty and pleasure. On the one side the obedient, and on the other the free. It seemed, and much against her better judgment she was forced to think about this, a straight division between the Christian and pagan worlds, and she had supposed that the one had merely superseded the other. Thus she constantly sought, and found, analogues in the real world, even in the little world of her diminished acquaintance, and she wondered if it were too late to learn the most important lesson of all: how to make it come out right in the end. So far she had found no reassurance.

Bringing her mind back to Patrick, she reflected that if she had married him she would certainly still be married to him, since he tended to read the same kind of fiction as she did. But she also saw that those evenings with the harp-sichords had exacted their forfeit: Patrick was now immovably a bachelor and would remain one whatever his marital status turned out to be. She doubted that he would ever marry or that he would ever want to. 'I loved you, Blanche,' he had said briefly when she told him of her forthcoming marriage. But she questioned whether his feelings were at all compatible with the sheer pragmatism of marriage, or whether he saw it, inaccurately, as a reflection of the divine harmony. She had never seen it that way herself: to her, marriage was a form of higher education, the kind that other women gained at universities. And she supposed that on her better days she would have got quite a good degree. Patrick, however, would expect her to get a First every day of the year. And knowing, as she knew now, the full extent of her ignorance, she was doubly relieved that she had not been put to the test.

'How lovely to see you,' she said. 'You must tell me all your news.'

And, he's gone, she thought. Bertie has gone. And felt a great grief before summoning up her most worldly smile.

Patrick, cautiously, saw that on the whole Blanche had not changed all that much, apart from an insubstantial loss of vitality: the same erect figure, the same distant air. He told himself that he must be wary of getting mixed up with her again. She meant no harm, having never been a calculating woman, but she must surely be lonely. He accepted a glass of wine from a bottle rather less than half full, thinking it odd that she did not offer him a glass of that very good sherry that he always remembered in this house. He noticed that the fringe of the rug was matted but that otherwise all was in order.

'But you look so well,' said Blanche vivaciously. 'Have you been away?'

'A few days in the Lake District, as usual,' he replied. 'Climbing.'

For even his holidays were strenuous and austere. Blanche saw in her mind's eye the dusty leaves of a palm tree in the public gardens in Nice, and herself, sitting on a bench, her face lifted blissfully to the sun. The sun is God, she thought, but she said, 'I need your advice, Patrick, about a young friend of mine.' So she is not in trouble, he thought, and prepared to listen.

In the telling, Sally's story seemed quite a straightforward affair, a simple matter of furnishing the right documents. She left out details such as Elinor's resistance to the situation but mentioned that the child had to stay with her grandmother because there was no money at home.

'Why don't they both do that?' asked Patrick.

Blanche said she thought this rather beside the point.

'It could be seen to be rather a valid point,' replied Patrick. This was not going well. Perhaps if she let Sally tell her story in her own way the outcome might be more successful. In any event she had done all she could and was now beginning to feel a certain weariness: she would rather Patrick and Sally settled matters between them, leaving her free to call on Sally occasionally but not to be bound to almost daily attendance. It has all been rather sad, she thought. And it is because I thought I could help the little girl. And perhaps thought she could help me.

'If you don't mind, Patrick, I'm going to telephone this friend right now, since I'm lucky enough to steal some of your time this evening.'

Patrick glanced at his watch.

'Now don't say you must be going. You would be doing me, I mean doing Sally, the most immense favour if you could just give her a word of advice. Face to face. And then I shall ask no more of you.

'Sally,' she said into the receiver. 'I've got a friend here who might be able to advise you. I think I mentioned him. Patrick Fox. I wonder, could you come round for a few minutes? I'm sure it would be worth your while. And then we can get it all sorted out.'

She hated the governessy sound of her own voice, hated the slight prickle of irritation she felt as she put down the telephone, hated what seemed to her to be the immensely difficult movement of social forces needed to bring together such unlikely conversationalists as Patrick Fox and Sally Beamish. She felt quite exhausted at the prospect of steering them through the evening. But she need not have worried. After half an hour, Sally came in lightly, wearing a strange dress of bitter green linen almost down to her ankles and held up by shoulder straps. She was unencumbered by the sort of paraphernalia that most women carry around with them, and although she must have had a key in her pocket – or had she simply left the door ajar? – her hands were empty. She trod noiselessly on her Roman sandals. Her vaguely unrealistic appearance was enhanced by her apparent weightlessness and by the familiarity with which she negotiated the obstacles of Blanche's drawing-room, which she had never previously visited. As Patrick rose slowly to his feet, with an expression of something like incredulity, Sally's face widened into an archaic smile. She sat down easily in a large chair and, still smiling, prepared to give him her full attention, as if he had to present his case to her rather than she to him. Blanche felt the beginnings of a slight headache.

Two hours later, when she was in the kitchen making sandwiches and coffee for the three of them, for the conversation had been terribly oblique and it seemed as if she could count on them both being there for hours yet, she wondered at the novelty of this populated evening, congratulating herself on the success of her enterprise. But much later she stole into her bedroom, while they were still talking, and, resting her head against the cold glass of the window, she strained her eyes to see out into the dark garden. It seemed to her then that there was something inalienable

97

about these night hours, these unseen musings. It was as though this essence of her being, this lonely child within her, this stolen solitude, this darkness, were all she had left, that the world of the day was for others, that she herself was a creature of the night, and that when she opened her curtains on to the cold purity of the sleeping earth she was performing an essential rite, or rather a rite essential to herself, and asserting her silence against the wilful authority of their sleepless babble.

S E V E N

Blanche's mother's other maxim had been, 'Do it now!'
Why this figured so largely in her entirely uneventful life
was difficult to say. But Blanche, marooned in even greater
idleness, had found it salutary. Unlike her mother, who
rarely got up before ten-thirty and changed her clothes two
or even three times a day, Blanche was ready, her strenuous
plans already laid, by nine-fifteen. By that time she had
performed the stoic task of getting up and was fully dressed,
her housework done, her newspaper briefly read, and even
her second cup of coffee a thing of the past. She felt vaguely
guilty at not having to have plans such as she supposed other
women to have: she would have had a quieter conscience if
she had had to go to work on a crowded bus, and to shop
for a family on the way home. She envied such women and
sometimes read recipe books to find out what she imagined
they were having for dinner. She herself ate without pleasure
or interest these days, and even the memory of the beautiful
meals she used to cook now seemed insubstantial, as if
divorce had cancelled them or reckoned them to be of
dwindling significance, like a lost reputation. The things she
ate these days – a single chop, an isolated Dover sole –
seemed to her rather more suitable subjects for still-life
painting than for consumption. They could be bought neg-
ligently, distastefully, and cooked in the same absent way.
She thought of titanic roasts of beef, hecatombs of vegetables,

puddings stuffed with fruit, trembling custards. For a brief period she had wondered whether, under pretext of helping out the mother, she could take Elinor home and cook her lunch, as she had done on two occasions, with varying success, but this plan had soon to be discarded. When together, Sally and Elinor appeared to live on spaghetti, toast, and green apples. Her offers of help had been laughed away; it seemed that she constantly misread the situation. If indigence required relief, it seemed that desire required satisfaction, and the two states were radically different, if not opposed. Blanche wished to contribute everything, including, if necessary, money. Sally's desire was for the restoration of luxury, ease, and entertainment. Unlike Blanche, who thought in terms of the present ('Do it now!'), Sally lived entirely in the past, a past which she wished to see reproduced, in identical form, in the future.

Sitting now in Sally's basement, with Patrick, and listening yet again to those stories of the past, embellished with reminiscent laughter, she wondered when Elinor would come home. As far as she could see, money was no longer the problem that it had been, since, in view of the fact that the situation was soon to be regularized, Blanche felt that it was only a matter of form to tide Sally over, as they both chose to think about it. It occurred to Blanche to wonder if Patrick did the same thing; being a man, she supposed he had a larger attitude to such matters, and he seemed to be taking a considerable measure of responsibility for the whole affair. 'Patrick said he might look in this evening,' Sally had said to her in a negligent far-away voice one afternoon, and Blanche had taken that to mean that her presence was not required. Yet it seemed that she was essential to Patrick's sense of propriety and he sometimes telephoned from his office and asked her to meet him there.

The behaviour of Patrick in this situation aroused Blanche's keenest interest but also her most melancholy memories. Both Patrick and Sally changed in each other's company, and Blanche's presence often seemed to her analogous to that of a duenna or a chaperone, giving an air of respectability to what might otherwise have seemed, to curious eyes, to be a *louche* assignation. In Patrick's company, and inevitably Blanche's too, Sally once again became the creature of those long-lost parties, sparkling as she never had for Blanche alone, and referring to a number of people whom Patrick seemed to know or at least to know of. Much of this anterior life of hers had been lived in the South of France or in Paris, where she had acquired most of her wardrobe; Patrick revealed a great interest in these regions, although, as far as Blanche knew, he tended to frequent more temperate climates and sterner scenery: Norway, the Grampians, the Hebrides. Sally was worldly, thought Blanche; she asserted her right to fascinate. In Patrick's presence she acquired whims, opinions, tastes, follies. She also established her claim to certain extravagances, which were always justified. Patrick assented to all this and thus made it seem doubly legitimate. Sally was either very acquisitive or very natural: Blanche could not quite decide which. Talking, as she did, of the past, she became airy, imponderable. Nurture had made her so. Whether, like Mousie, she had been the object of her father's indulgence, or whether her mysteriously absent husband, with his romantic but slightly moist good looks, had lavished on her the full force of his adoration, Sally had the achieved air of one who has always been within her rights. In this she was more advanced than Mousie but recognizably of the same family.

There was within Sally a kind of readiness for friendship, but for a friendship based essentially on amusement. She was not inclined to, or stimulated by, acts of altruism. Blanche could see that her feeling for Elinor was based on a certain spasmodic camaraderie; and that was why the child, to a limited extent, trusted her. What the child resisted was precisely her pleasure-loving insubstantiality, her desire to be diverted, her readiness to accept the next invitation, her availability. Blanche saw that as a mother, or as a putative mother, Sally was indeed nymph-like; she would provide a temporary shelter for the little girl and educate her to a sort of viability, but it would be senseless to demand of her further guidance. At the age of seven Elinor would be expected to be self-reliant; at the age of ten she would be given her sexual education; at the age of fifteen or sixteen she would be expected to have left home for good. Her refusal to speak was based on her foreknowledge of this fate.

Thus the whole principle of generation would be undersold, for Sally would never yield her place. Her place was to be young and to be the centre of attention. Mothers like this, as Blanche knew only too well, induce bewilderment, loneliness. For this reason she thought of Mrs Duff, who was childless and who had once been seen by Blanche to have real tears in her eyes when admiring a baby outside the Post Office. Blanche, on her way to the hospital that day, had greeted her neighbour as usual, and then taken her arm in concern. 'Mrs Duff,' she had said. 'Are you all right?' Mrs Duff, at this abstract and routine kindness, had applied a snowy handkerchief to her eyes. 'It's just that I so wanted one of my own,' she whispered. 'And now it's too late.' Yes, thought Blanche, you would have been a good mother, always concerned, always delighted. The arrangements seemed to her random and slapdash. The cruelty of the world in apportioning children to the wrong mothers plunged her briefly into a kind of mourning, which she modestly added to all the others.

And yet Sally Beamish clearly thought her a fortunate woman, and Patrick too, for all she knew. They saw that she was well provided for and not in need of assistance. She was aware that her reticence in the matter of the complaints she might have imagined herself entitled to make caused her to seem very dull. She never talked about her husband and was thus judged to be unfeeling. She guarded her memories, which were becoming ever more fragile, and was thus dismissed as uncommunicative. If she figured at all in their vocabulary, she thought, it must be as if she were surrounded by a penumbra of vagueness, and always designated by her money, either by the possession of it (which removed any concern for her) or by her ability to disburse it (which made her tiresome but necessary). Any obduracy in her character would be put down to meanness, whereas it was in fact the sum total of several resolves, some of them of a heroic nature.

And Patrick, who had once thought her precious, or so she supposed, now viewed her with indifference and exhibited an eagerness bordering on fatuity when, seated in the ruined brown Fifties chair, and watching Sally disposing her full length on the *chaise-longue*, he chose to assess her situation by indulging his curiosity about her past. Blanche supposed that he did not meet too many women of Sally's persuasion, and that her very lack of all the qualities he possessed excited his thoughts, offering him, as it were, an unusual holiday, with implications of luxury that he was simply unable to imagine on his own. Blanche could see that no impropriety had taken place, but she could also see that it was in the air, was indeed the very essence of the confrontation. Sally, with practised nonchalance, with elemental expertise, baited Patrick on his sedentary ordered life; Patrick rose delightedly to her teasing, and very soon, and almost habitually, they were exchanging remarks of so unserious and irrelevant a nature that Blanche gazed out of the window and thought that, were it not for her desire to see Elinor again, she would abandon them both and disappear for ever from this basement.

This had now happened on two separate occasions since Blanche had introduced Patrick to Sally, two evenings spent listening to the kind of flirtatious remarks that were, on Sally's part, a reassertion of her own skills, a simple recall of modes of conversation useful in the past, and on Patrick's, a delighted if cautious acceptance of this, to him, new method of discourse. It was on the third occasion, when a telephone call from Sally, asking her to come round and to contact Patrick at the same time, had prepared her for another wasted evening, that the situation appeared to have changed. Arriving first, in answer to this summons, she had found Sally looking uncharacteristically moody, having reverted to her former clouded indifference, and it occurred to her that something must have happened, that the present must once again have managed to occlude the past, bringing with it its usual freight of boredom and disenchantment. Information was once again vague, and an indifference had settled on the down-drooping features. When Patrick arrived, with, Blanche saw thankfully, a bottle of wine, Sally summoned up the energy to sparkle briefly at him and then lapsed into an unfamiliar thoughtfulness, gazing intently out of the window, and lifting and smoothing the hair on the nape of her neck as Blanche had once seen her doing at the hospital. After a few minutes of this a tension was set up, and Blanche saw that Patrick had no means of dealing with it.

'Sally,' she said. 'Is anything wrong?'

Sally sighed. 'Paul's coming home,' she said. 'Next week.'

'But that's splendid,' cried Blanche.

'Is it? Not this time, apparently.'

'But why not?' asked Blanche. 'What is the problem?'

'The problem is . . .' Sally lit another cigarette. 'The problem is that he hasn't got any money. The problem *is*', she took a deep drag on her cigarette, 'that the charming Mr Demuth won't pay him.'

'I don't understand,' said Blanche. 'Why not?'

'Because he says that Paul owes him money.'

It was now Patrick's turn to say, 'I don't understand.'

'Well, obviously Paul has had to have expenses. He can't live on nothing. Neither of us can. He may have drawn on Demuth's account. Nothing wrong with that – he would have paid it back. But Demuth's now saying that Paul has embezzled money from him. The cheek of it. And apparently they're all coming over, all three of them, and Demuth is threatening to sue Paul, and I don't know what's going to happen.'

She sighed again, apparently with boredom. There was a silence, as Blanche and Patrick struggled, in their different ways, to accommodate this information. Blanche, to her surprise, was not shocked: she had suspected from the first that something unusual was going on, that a profound irregularity underlay the superficial irregularity of Sally's life. Patrick appeared to be more shaken, not so much by the evidence of Paul's crime, if crime it was, as by the effect it was bound to have on Sally.

'My dear girl,' he said. 'My dear girl.' Then his expression became uneasy as he appeared to wonder how he had become embroiled in this situation and what he might be asked to accomplish if he were to be allowed out of it.

'I don't see how either of us can help,' said Blanche, acknowledging defeat, a defeat which she had not anticipated.

'Perhaps I could see the letter?' Patrick's voice had already become more constrained, more official.

Sally, with small brown fingers looking quite useless for practical purposes, handed him a letter headed 'Ritz Hotel', and covered with dashing slanting writing so racy, so urgent, that it was almost illegible. Patrick, who saw with relief that he could hardly decipher it, handed it over thankfully to Blanche. Blanche managed to read one line, '. . . hanging on to your coat, which he says is his by right . . .', and then only isolated words, 'monster', 'insult', 'my poor angel'. He signed weakly, but with massive underlinings, 'your Paul'. She placed the letter carefully on the trolley, said, 'Excuse me a moment,' went out into the kitchen, and placed three ten-pound notes under the lid of the teapot. She knew perfectly well that this was a futile and masochistic gesture, her only way of quieting a conscience that refused to be engaged any further. It was clear to her that Paul must have been sending money home, that this money was not his to send, and that his employer had now found him out. There may even have been other extravagances, of which they knew nothing. Sally had said that Paul enjoyed high living, and his romantic looks carried a message of unreliability. But romantic looks so often do, she reproached herself. That is why they are romantic. And a very good case could be made out for Paul. Supposing this Demuth is too suspicious? Supposing Paul was keeping strict accounts, and that they would have reckoned the whole thing up at the end, what was owing and what was not? Supposing Paul is the sort of man who insists on buying luxuries for his wife, despite her protestations? Supposing he was sending her what he thought were his wages? Except that he wasn't being paid wages; only expenses. And that argues that they were keeping him on a tight rein, that they had reason to watch him.

But where does Mrs Demuth come into all this? Surely a middle-aged woman would plead for a young man with Paul's looks and apparent charm? Unless ... But there must be a limit to the squalor of her imaginings, for the precise form of which, however, there were precedents both classical and Biblical. None of this, she knew, could be elucidated by Sally, who had now reverted to the discontented trailing silences, her rare sentences left unfinished, that she had formerly manifested in Blanche's presence. Patrick's smile had faded; his flirtatious proposals were quite in abeyance. Suddenly Blanche was aware that he was a middle-aged man, putting on weight, no longer as eligible in appearance as he once had been, and, she saw, unequal to this situation. She felt, along with a great weariness, an immense distaste, not for Patrick, not even for Sally, but for herself. She had thought that she could do some good, both to herself and to this little family, and she had done less than was even necessary. She had thought to be of service, as befits the fallen creation, and all the while she had been fascinated, like a spy, by the freedom of those who are not bound by rules. Her contributions, though serviceable, had been in every sense inadequate. And throughout this imbroglio she had been without dignity. It was this that shamed and hurt her. Her pitiful intentions had led her into stupidity. And, she realized, she had been misled by the archaic smile and all its implications into betraying her true nature. She determined to have no more of it.

'I must go,' she said, perhaps a little abruptly. Patrick looked up in surprise.

'Blanche has been a brick,' said Sally, glancing at her pensively. 'Don't worry about us. Patrick will sort something out. It's just that I felt a bit fraught this evening.' She paused. 'Particularly with Nellie coming home the day after tomorrow.'

Ah yes, thought Blanche, stopping for a tiny moment in her progress to the door. Of course. There are resources still to be deployed. But she said goodnight and left.

The night was humid and uneasy, a storm brewing somewhere. She walked the few streets to her house lost in thoughts of an incoherent nature. It occurred to her that she had never been deceived; merely surprised. Eternally surprised by the appetites of others and the lengths to which these appetites would take them. And she had been naive enough to think of this trait as selfishness, when it was life itself in its brutal urgings and promptings. It was the lesson she had never learned, being too schooled and educated in careful manners, and hoping to win her reward by scrupulous good faith. Yet always increasingly aware of the appetites of others, now as palpable as the thunder rolling in the distance and the storm that would, at some unspecified time, but inevitably, break.

In her bedroom she lit a single lamp, undressed, and, standing at the window and looking out over the garden, willed herself into a state of calm. Numbly she acknowledged the fact that all her efforts led towards sadness. For that reason she had no way of knowing whether or not they were valid. She supposed her sadness to be a matter of temperament or rather an accident of birth, as if, in some gigantic lottery, it had been decided that she were to be denied the enjoyment of her own free will. And the irony of it was that she had been unaware of this fact until she was middle-aged. As a child, like all children, she had felt that the world was as much hers as anybody else's; and as a grown woman she had had no reason to doubt her happy state. It was only recently that the truth had begun to become clear to her, as if only just coming into focus. It was now that she saw the superior freedom of others. The unease felt at the National Gallery, the curious faintness that had overcome her at the sight of the archaic smile of the kouros in the Athens Museum, seemed to her to be an essential commentary on her own shortcomings. I could have saved my own life, she thought. But I was too weak, shackled by the wrong mythology.

She took down from her shelves a classical dictionary that had belonged to her grandfather and turned to the section on Hercules. This brute, this bully had performed actions that were accounted miracles in the ancient world. These actions were popularly known as the Twelve Labours, but now she found that there were more, as if they had proliferated in his wake. In his cradle he had crushed the heads of two serpents sent by Juno to strangle him. As a youth he impregnated the fifty daughters of Thespius in a single night,

108

'which brought him fifty Boyes'. He destroyed the monster Hydra; he caught and killed the hind with brazen feet. In the Nemean forest he slew a lion that was not to be hurt by iron, wood or stone. He vanquished Diomedes, King of Thrace, and fed him to his horses. He slew the Erymanthian boar; he shot the Stymphalian birds; he tamed the wild bull of Crete. He vanquished his rival Achelous in a combat for his mistress Deianeira. He slew Busiris, King of Egypt. He strangled, in a wrestling match, the giant Antaeus. He, most beautifully, carried off the golden apples of the Hesperides. He conquered Geryon, King of Spain, and took away his herds of fat cattle. He beat out the brains of Cacus, who, like his father, Vulcan, vomited tongues of flame. He slew Lacinius and on the place of his triumph built a temple to Juno, called Juno Lacinia. He tamed the Centaurs. He cleansed the Augean stables. He delivered Hesione from the sea monster. He conquered the Queen of the Amazons. He went down into Hell and brought back Cerberus on a triple chain. With his arrow he shot the eagle that was feeding on the still-growing liver of Prometheus. He killed Cygnus, in a duel on horseback. He slew the winged sons of Boreas. He passed the torrid zone and the burning sands of Libya, and waded through the quicksands of the Syrtes. He slew Eurythus, King of Oechalia, and carried off the Princess Iole. This, however, was his undoing, for when Deianeira heard of it she sent him a poisoned shirt which led to his death. Then, read Blanche, 'After his death he was held a god, and believed to be the same as the sun'. So the sun *is* God, she thought.

All through that dark night she thought of this, and much else besides. In the morning she dressed carefully and went to the hospital, as usual. It was one of her days there, and she saw no reason to change it. She worked conscientiously, left for home in the late afternoon, and bought herself a bottle of Meursault to drink when she got there.

Bathed and changed, she sat and waited for Bertie, although he had not said that he would come. Nevertheless, she expected him. She knew him to be on the brink of his Greek holiday and supposed that he would look in to say goodbye to her. It occurred to her that these visits were, from his point of view, not really necessary. It was a year since the divorce and she had still not gone on the rampage, so there could hardly be any need for him to keep up this rather wary form of supervision. And as she had never heaped reproaches on his head – although she had never gone to much trouble to hide her dislike of Mousie – she supposed that he came back out of solicitude, to see how she was getting on. She did not think that she was stimulating company these days, for she assumed that sadness had dimmed her wit: therefore she took care to look nice for him and to provide some refreshment.

'You are the only person I know who thinks that cake is an accompaniment to wine,' he said, helping himself. 'This is rather good. Lemon?'

'It neutralizes the acid,' said Blanche. 'And you can drink so much more if there is something to mop it up. Wine, in my opinion, is wasted on a meal.'

'And what have you been doing with yourself?' asked Bertie, leaning back comfortably and brushing crumbs from his shirt.

'Bertie,' said Blanche. 'You look terrible. You need a haircut, and that shirt would look loud on a juvenile. There is no need to let yourself go, you know. When one is middle-aged, it behooves one to look one's best.'

'It behooves one, does it? Let me tell you, Blanche, I have more than enough to do these days without ogling myself in the glass every five minutes.'

'That is hardly my fault, is it? Anyway, what do you do that is so arduous? What have you done today, for example, except to put on that absurd shirt, in Fulham, and drive to the office? Have you been down to Hell and brought back Cerberus on a triple chain? Have you shot the Stymphalian birds? Have you delivered Hesione from the sea monster? Have you impregnated the fifty daughters of Thespius?'

'Certainly not,' said Bertie. 'Is there another bottle of this?'

'In a minute. It occurs to me, Bertie, that your life is rather easy, compared with that of Hercules.'

'And why should I compare my life with that of Hercules?'

'Because he proves that you can get away with murder and still be admired for it.'

'And you think that I have got away with murder?' asked Bertie, thinking, This is it. This is what I got away with, and perhaps what I have come back for. He had been preparing himself for such a confrontation and now that it had come, so late in the day, he had completely forgotten what it was he had meant to say. His careful arguments, many of them augmented by Mousie, had simply slipped away from him.

'I suppose you have done what most men think of doing and what many men actually do. And I grant you that it must have taken some courage. You are a conventional man, Bertie, and you hate fuss.'

Bertie, who had got more fuss than he bargained for, sighed.

'I can see', said Blanche, with heightened colour, 'that I am a limited woman. Or rather, a woman with limited appeal. I suppose I am rather careful, and you once called me stately. Not one of those nudging giggling women who seem to make such an impression on men. Except that I thought you were too intelligent to put up with that. I was wrong. It was what you wanted. Perhaps you never wanted me much in the first place.'

'Oh yes,' said Bertie. 'I wanted you all right.'

'But you left me.'

Bertie sighed. 'I wanted to start again. It was as simple as that. I wanted to go through it all again, the excitement, the anxiety, even the upheaval. It was exhilarating. To tell the truth, since we are telling the truth, I didn't expect to *have* to leave you. It was Mousie who...'

'Ah, yes. And you didn't think that might happen? In your exhilaration?'

'I rather thought you might have understood it. You always understood *me*.'

'I have just told you how much I understand you. And perhaps I would have condoned it if I hadn't felt so disgraced. Those awful friends of yours thinking what a lark it all was and inviting you both to dinner. I divorced *them* as much as you. I thought I could manage better without all those reminders.'

'And can you? Manage better, I mean.'

'No,' she said. 'No, I can't. I don't think I can manage at all. I think I have become more foolish since you left me. The only company I have is that of virtuous matrons or whatever lame dogs I happen to acquire. I have become reduced to somebody who is supposed to occupy herself with good works. Not that I am opposed to that, but I sometimes have the feeling that somebody else would do them if I didn't. And it is so terrible to come back to an empty house. I can't tell you how terrible it is. Of course, I have all those wonderful resources that people keep telling me about. There is always the National Gallery,' she said, blowing her nose. 'And somehow I am expected to manage on my own. I don't know why this is. I am expected to do without holidays or birthdays or Christmas or all those things that real three-dimensional people have. I am expected not to *expect* them.'

'You could marry again,' he said, watching her carefully. 'Barbara tells me that you have been seeing something of Patrick Fox.'

'Patrick? Are you suggesting that I should marry Patrick?'

'He was always very fond of you.'

'Patrick? How could I marry Patrick when I am still in love with you?'

They looked at each other in amazement.

'Bertie,' said Blanche. 'Don't come here again. It is too easy for you to look in and conclude that I am all right. And it makes it easier for me to know that I might see you again. But I don't think you can come back, not after this evening. I shall have to have the courage not to know about you.'

'And I about you?'

'I can't help it,' she said. 'We must abide by the agreement. All it needs is a little strength.'

'But you have just told me that I am no Hercules.'

'You wouldn't want his record. Think of your conscience.'

'I can't say goodbye, Blanche.'

'Yes, you can. You've said it once.' But, she thought, it is the second time that kills.

Eventually she closed the door behind him, and stood for a moment, looking at the shattered cake that he had so enjoyed. And I forgot to open that second bottle, she thought, and sat down and wept.

EIGHT

'So when she said she was going to Cornwall with her sister, I made no demur.' Miss Elphinstone spoke from the doorway of the drawing-room, duster in one hand, silver candlestick in another. 'Well, I wasn't going to argue with her. I just gave her to understand that I couldn't comment. What I can't appreciate, I ignore.'

Blanche listened half-heartedly, although apparently giving Miss Elphinstone her full attention. Now if ever was the time to summon up her famous resources. The summer was advancing, revealing its empty side to those who stayed at home. Each morning the sun, blanketed in white mist, rose over the garden and hovered uncertainly for the rest of the day, before blazing with sudden intensity at about five o'clock, encouraging thoughts of settled weather. But the weather remained unsettled, with unusually high rainfall, which Blanche heard crepitating on the leaves of the garden in the early dawn. She rose in a daze of tiredness, her mind empty of thought, to face a day whose demands seemed to increase rather than to disappear with habit. Postcards arrived from absent friends. Barbara and Jack, about to depart for their cottage, telephoned with instructions about feeding the cats while they were away. Blanche imagined Bertie in Greece.

'And what will you do with yourself while I'm away, Blanche?' enquired Miss Elphinstone. 'Mark you, I'll only

be gone the week. Just give you time to miss me, won't I?'
And she flashed Blanche a smile of great kindness before
turning away to pack her leather hold-all, her rubber gloves
carefully folded around her holiday money, and a freshly
baked cherry cake, Blanche's going away present, poised
delicately on the top.

This would be a tedious day. Blanche supposed that she
should telephone Sally but found herself curiously unwilling
to do so. This little adventure had run its course, and perhaps
Patrick was the one who could best steer it to some sort of
conclusion. She felt a passing sadness at her own inadequacy
but retained enough common sense to know that in this
particular situation the complications would simply pro-
liferate. It seemed to her that no one in Sally's entourage
had the brutality to engage her fully in the problems of the
present. In any event, the focus of attention must now not
be Sally but her mysterious husband, whom Blanche had no
desire to meet. I really only wanted to know Elinor, she
thought; her parents were necessary footnotes, whilst Elinor
was the main concern. And now I don't suppose that I shall
see her again. Out of her pervading sorrow, she thought
with sadness of the child.

It was in the early afternoon, when Miss Elphinstone had
left, and a silence had fallen on the house, and on the street
outside, that the telephone rang. 'Why, hello, Blanche,' said
Sally warmly. 'How are you?' Blanche murmured that she
was well. 'Nellie and I were wondering if you could come
to tea today. Nellie's longing to see you,' said Sally. There
was a specious brightness about her voice that Blanche perceived over and above the proffered invitation. It was as if
Sally were disturbed in some way and was translating this
disturbance into the habit of thought that came most easily
to her: blitheness. Simultaneously, Blanche recognized this
blitheness with a certain amount of dread. The old feeling
of fear instilled itself into her mind again. Somehow her

contact with Sally was experienced as a loss of her own competence, for behind that blitheness lay requirements which she would be expected to meet without ever quite knowing what they were. Having marked Blanche down as inadequate to her purposes, Sally had perforce to make use of her. Blanche was quite aware of this. Her fear came in part from the feeling of being ruthlessly pursued and partly from an older feeling, and for an instant she saw in her mind's eye the dream that she had had: herself, with white feathers in her hair, pulling on the oars of a rowing boat, while her mother, dressed in beige chiffon, looked on amused. But this is ridiculous, she told herself; no one is pursuing me. It may even be that I am lending myself to this, just as I did to Mother's little manoeuvres, which could be the meaning of the white feathers. But she knew that she had dreamed the dream in the first place, and that she was thinking about it now because she had felt she was the one who needed rescuing, and that she had been reduced to this galley-slave behaviour only by the indifference of others.

Sally, she was aware, was quite indifferent to her. She was neither amusing enough, indiscreet enough, nor indeed rich enough to share any serious confidences with her. Sally regarded her as an extremely distant outpost of the welfare services, and was no doubt imprinted with this belief because she had first met Blanche at the hospital. Sally probably regarded the offerings left under the lid of the teapot as some kind of official contribution to her predicament and had not questioned it, indeed would not even dream of questioning it. She regarded this strange hiatus in her fortunes as some kind of accident, for which the influence of Saturn or some other cosmic configuration was to blame. Her main concern was to live through it unencumbered by responsibility, in order to move on smoothly to happier times with the least possible inconvenience. Blanche could see that when the time came for her to move on she would leave no trace behind, as if indeed her footprints were as weightless as those of the nymphs or dryads she so closely resembled.

The child was a different matter. The child was earthbound. From the first moment of seeing her, pushing her cake around her plate with the hospital's shiny metal teaspoon, Blanche knew that Elinor had already learned difficulty and pain. The blitheness of the mother had merely increased the seriousness of the little girl. Blanche now saw that Sally's most worrying feature was her lack of gravity, although she might be concerned enough about her own expectations. On the other hand Elinor seemed to have no expectations of any sort, as if even growing up were almost too difficult for her, as if, at three years old, or a little older, she was more burdened than her mother could ever be. And this difference in temperament, stemming no doubt from the genetic disposition of her real mother, who had given up and died, opposed her implacably to Sally, who had the misleading facility of a woman who could do anything, but who lacked the wistfulness that betrays the woman who loves children.

The absent Paul Blanche had long dismissed as a lightweight, as a lighter weight than his wife. The boyish good looks she remembered from his photograph had become converted in her mind to an impression of pleading, hesitancy, embarrassment. From a distance she sensed the man's plausibility. She saw in those moist shining eyes the good-looking young romantic who had fallen in love with Sally and swept her off her feet with presents and luxuries, in the same way as he had swept all difficulties out of the way, relegating his infant daughter to his mother's care, and living the life of a stateless person, without responsibilities, until, under threat of insolvency, and no doubt as a joke, he had taken on a job with this ridiculous American to whom he would lend his services for a year in order to make enough money to disappear once more, with Sally, to live a life of play. The fact that this play was invisible, anonymous, abroad, and conducted with the assistance of an instant 'crowd', made it seem all the more unreal, yet at the same time more legendary. Blanche thought that the husband was probably rather uninteresting, inferior to his wife, and forced into ever more daring or outrageous enterprises in order to retain her attention. He might even be aware that her attention was wandering, and was probably, under the guise of boyish ardour, terrified.

As she walked out into the hazy sunshine, which seemed to surround her like a sparkling mist and drew out earthy vapours from shrubs and bushes that were already taking on the darker green of midsummer, Blanche reflected that while she had been seated modestly on her bench in the public gardens, under the shade of a dusty palm, Sally and her friends were no doubt waking late in the Carlton or the Negresco or the Martinez or whatever happened to be the hotel of the moment in the resort of the day after a party which had no doubt gone on until dawn. My pleasures were always too modest, thought Blanche, for it is immodesty that wins concessions. I sat there, in those gardens, face blissfully uplifted, knowing that in an hour I should go back to the hotel and see Bertie, and counting that moment more than adequate recompense for the strenuous public evening I should be forced to undergo, being witty in a restaurant with his friends. And no doubt, at the same time, in a similar restaurant, Sally and her friends were preparing for another sleepless night, but being younger did not feel the strain of putting on this evening performance. And perhaps in the daytime, when I got up early to walk on those pristine sands, I may have been marking out the spot where she and her friends, groaning, would lie down later in the day. She is the sort of woman men admire, and her entertainments are more suited to their taste than my poor pastimes. That is why I never speak to her of my own holidays in the south;

I avoid the reflections that my confidences would give rise to, both in her mind and in mine. I avoid the confrontation.

Blanche was well aware that in her mind she had already made the dangerous comparison between Sally and Mousie and between Elinor and herself. She saw this not so much as a struggle between vice and virtue – for she apportioned herself much the lesser role in all this – as between effectiveness and futility or between vitality and inertia. And somewhere in the middle of these conflicting principles, she saw the man, uncommitted, easily beguiled, *volage*. She saw also that her visits to the National Gallery, which had been designed to rescue her from a noisome self-pity, had simply brought these principles into focus and into opposition. On the one hand she had seen the fallen creation and its mournful effigies – the bleached virgins, the suffering saints, the un-called-for martyrdoms – and on the other the carefree mythological excesses of those who did not, or did not need to, know of the alternative convention. It seemed to her now that those mocking smiles had brought her to this point in her life, and that after saying goodbye to Bertie yet again she had consigned herself to the order which she continually questioned. At this very moment, while she was walking down this little street, becalmed in its afternoon quiet and reverting in appearance to the suburb it had once been, Bertie might be worshipping the sun god, on that island where surely some rout awaited him. Even now she could see, some way ahead of her, Mrs Duff, that embodiment of heavenly duty and obedience, proud with the pride of her legitimate wifely concerns, unvisited by subversive thoughts, and happily subdued by the bonds of matrimonial felicity.

Her encounters with the pagans (for that was how she now thought of them, although well aware of the distortion) had brought her to this modest pass. She walked carefully down the tree-lined street, in careful grey sandals, with yet another cake in her shopping bag. So abstracted were her thoughts that she passed her neighbour with no more than an abstracted smile, and, as an after-image, saw the eager words fade on Mrs Duff's lips. Walking down the steps to Sally's basement, she took one last long breath of the river-laden, dust-laden air, and rang the bell, to find the door opened instantly by Sally, wearing what looked like a long sleeveless marigold-coloured vest, belted loosely around the hips, and Elinor, who, having seen her, immediately retreated into the gloom of the sitting-room.

'Nellie!' cried Sally, laughing. 'Come here at once! You remember Mrs Vernon, don't you? She brought you that lovely book about trains.'

Elinor stood still, in the middle of the room, considering the matter. She appeared older, taller, slightly altered. Staying with her grandmother seemed to have shaken her hitherto unshakeable confidence, and after a moment she went to Sally and took her hand.

'I don't know,' said Sally, still laughing. 'She's forgotten all about us, I think. She doesn't know where she is. She keeps following me, and she never used to do that.' She stooped down to the child and pinched her chin. 'She's afraid I might send her away again, I suppose. Not that there's much hope of keeping her here,' she added in an aside to Blanche. 'Not with what we've got on the *tapis* at the moment.'

'Well, darling,' said Blanche, also stooping to the child, and meeting her hesitant and unresponsive gaze. 'Did you have a nice time?' No reply, of course; nothing had changed. 'And is it nice being home with Sally again?' Elinor turned her head away from these promptings, and seeing Blanche's shopping basket wandered over to it and began to look inside. When she found the cake, she turned to Blanche questioningly, and, on receiving a nod, lifted it carefully on to a chair and began to undo the waxed paper in which it was wrapped. I forgot to bring her a present, Blanche thought regretfully, and this thought was evidently shared by Elinor, who, having uncovered the cake, pushed it away and ran out of the room. 'Elinor,' said Blanche, blushing at the hideousness of the remark. 'There's a gold coin hidden somewhere in my purse. Do you think you can find it? It can buy you a present when Sally takes you to the shops tomorrow.' Elinor came slowly back into the room, took Blanche's bag, and, turning over and rejecting wallet, diary and handkerchief, found the little mesh purse that Bertie had bought in an antique shop, long ago, and occupied herself with the contents. Soon, five gold coins had been carefully put on one side. Sally, coming in with the Danish silver teapot, laughed. 'Just like her father,' she said. 'She's fearfully excited about Paul coming home, aren't you? When are we going to see Daddy?' she asked. Elinor went to the photograph of her father and kissed it. The child has been corrupted, thought Blanche, and immediately winced at the unkindness of the thought.

They sat down to the watery tea in the riveted flowered cups, Elinor in her small chair, Blanche's cake, forgotten in its paper, on the seat of another.

'Have you seen him yet?' asked Blanche.

'No.' No shadow seemed to interfere with Sally's mirth.

'He's still closeted in the Dorchester with the Demuths. He's telephoned, of course.'

'Can't you go to the Dorchester and see him?'

'Well, I can't leave Nellie. And I can't take her with me because the things we have to discuss are definitely *not* for her ears.' Sally laughed.

'I could take care of her if you want to . . .'

'Sweet of you, but that's not actually what's needed. No, what's actually needed is someone to go and talk to the Demuths. Tell them what a splendid chap Paul is and how he's never going to be naughty again.'

Blanche placed her cup very carefully back in its saucer.

'And who could do that?' she asked.

'Well, you could, for a start, Blanche.'

'Are you serious, Sally? I've never even met your husband.'

'Well, you know us. And you're a person in good standing. No, Nellie, you can't have that cake. That cake belongs to Blanche.'

'But Sally, how could I possibly talk to the Demuths, whom I've also never met, and tell them Paul is splendid, when from what I gather he *has* been what you call naughty?'

'All right,' said Sally airily. 'It was just a thought. Forget it. We'll work something out.' And, taking the child on to her knee, she said, 'Did I ever tell you about that time we ran out of money in Cannes? What a hoot *that* was.' And on it came again, the story of Sally's inexhaustible anterior life in the South of France, with full complement of reminiscent laughter interrupted only by kisses given to Elinor, who relaxed in her mother's arms, her eyes regarding Blanche incuriously, her small hand on Sally's marigold-coloured knee. 'Only that time there were friends to bail us out. Otherwise we'd still be there. Wouldn't we?' she said to Elinor. Elinor, unexpectedly, smiled.

This is torture, thought Blanche, torture by infinite recall. She is going to tell me all about her holidays and parties and what fun she had before she had the misfortune to be translated here until I beg for mercy. She will do this until I consent to go and see these Demuths, which she seems to think is a matter of no moment at all, the sort of errand that dull people like myself can most usefully be sent on. Until I agree to do this she will continue to belabour me with this monologue which is cleverly disguised as conversation. Perhaps she is really very unhappy and all this talk is a kind of fugue, a clinical flight from the present. But, looking at Sally, fresh-faced and relaxed in her modish garb, Blanche found it difficult to believe that this was true. Far more worrying than Sally, whose apparent lightheartedness might even be frighteningly real, was the inertia of the child, her new obedience, her fatigue. Even now her eyes were sleepily closing. Here, Blanche thought, was a reaction she could understand, the dreadful drowsiness that comes with grieving, the black sleep that overtakes one almost without warning, so that one wakes with a dry mouth and contorted limbs, wondering what day it is. But Sally, who is indifferent to, no, almost empowered by, the hazards of this situation, which remind her of other hazards, successfully overcome, though by what means I cannot know, may be that rare thing, a delinquent personality. She may thrive on the excitement of close shaves, ill-gotten gains, flights to freedom, escapes of all sorts. Truly weightless, like the characters in mythology. And, like them, unscrupulous.

'Sally,' she said. 'You do see that I couldn't possibly go and talk to the Demuths, don't you? As I say, I don't know them, I've never met Paul, and it does sound to me as if he's been a little unwise. I think it's something he'll have to put right himself.'

Sally shrugged. 'I just thought it might be something you were good at. After all, your husband was a diplomat, wasn't he?'

Blanche stared at her. 'Whatever gave you that idea? My husband is an estate agent.'

'Well, why didn't you *say* so?'

'It didn't seem relevant,' said Blanche humbly.

Sally pealed with laughter, shaking Elinor from her somnolence.

'And here was I thinking you were frightfully grand,' she said.

Blanche told herself that the girl was merely tactless, although she knew herself to be hurt, not by Sally's misconception but by her utter lack of curiosity. How could she believe such a thing if she did not even know that it was

123

true? And how could she compute a quality as being of potential use to her when it was based on nothing more than a hazy impression in her own mind? Frightfully grand, indeed. Not that she believed that, Blanche knew. What she thought she saw was the power of money. She thought that not only the money could help her but the power as well. All utterly illusory.

'Anyway,' Sally went on. 'I'm quite sure you're grand enough for the Demuths. They won't know the difference.'

'Ah, but I will,' said Blanche, her colour rather high. 'I'm not sure that the Demuths are my problem, you know. If Paul has caused some embarrassment, then I think it is up to him to make amends.'

'It's just that it would look better if someone spoke on his behalf. I got the impression you were rather fond of us, that's all. You seem to like coming here.'

Blanche looked round the room, saw her unwanted cake on the seat of a chair, saw Elinor's somnolescent gaze, saw her hand on Sally's knee, saw her indifference.

'You know I am fond of you both,' she said. 'But what inducement could I hold out on Paul's behalf to the Demuths? After all, they know him and I don't. It would be dishonest . . .'

'Oh, dishonest,' said Sally. 'I thought you might do it for Nellie, that's all.'

'Why don't *you* do it for her?' asked Blanche.

'The Demuths would take more notice of someone like you,' said Sally. 'Someone older,' she added.

There was a short silence. Do it now, Blanche thought. 'I don't think I can help you,' she said, quite firmly. 'If you want the advice of someone older, have you thought of asking Patrick? Although I'm sure, knowing him as I do, that he would say that Paul must be responsible.'

'Well, Patrick's trouble is that he doesn't want to get involved. I'm speaking generally, of course. I haven't asked him about this. But I can see that he's one of those frightened inhibited men who're dreadfully hung up about sex.'

'Sex doesn't come into this,' said Blanche.

'No, I'm speaking generally. He's fascinated by it and he runs a mile when he sees it coming. No, Patrick's got his own problems. In fact, he's a problem all on his own. He said he might look in this evening, by the way.'

Her features had begun to droop once more, giving her a look of distaste and fatigue. Elinor was fast asleep. It looked to Blanche as if they might both stay in this abandoned position until rescued. A fly, she saw, had settled on the cake.

'Perhaps you could mention it to him then,' she said, rising to go.

An air of dereliction settled over the room, which began to resemble the palace of the Sleeping Beauty. Sally and Elinor, both, in their different attitudes, quite motionless, ignored Blanche, as it would seem for ever. Dirty cups, Elinor's little pile of coins, the hapless cake, spoke mutely of useless stratagems. At the door Blanche glanced back. Sally, shifting the sleeping child on her lap, lifted a languid hand in farewell.

This will not do, said Blanche to herself, striding fiercely along pavements made dusty by the sudden five o'clock sunshine, and, Something must be done. I cannot turn up at the Dorchester and confront these strangers, making an eloquent nineteenth-century plea on behalf of widows and orphans. Patrick will have to do it; maybe it will help him overcome his inhibitions. Maybe this is just what the doctor ordered. Where are all the social workers now that we need them? It cannot be that I am the only person in the world capable of performing this action, an action which is both dubious and duplicitous. At the Dorchester, of all places. Appealing to a man so remote that he has to hire someone to do his talking for him. Which is almost what Sally has done with me, of course. Appealing to Mrs Demuth to release the impounded red fox coat. Making a fool of myself to save another woman's fur coat. It is my own fault, of course. Did I really think she wanted me for my dull company? And was I entirely innocent in seeking hers? But I am afraid I rather admire her. In her way she is admirable. She is not even a bad mother; look how Elinor clung to her today. All this nonsensical thinking, dividing people into two categories, and my longing to know more about the one from which I am excluded, has driven me slightly mad. And Elinor's hands were dirty; she is only a little girl, innocent of all this. But knowing about it, all the same.

'Patrick,' she said into the telephone. 'I understand that you're dropping in to see Sally this evening. I wonder if you could come on to me afterwards. I could give you an omelette. We ought to have a talk. Something must be done.'

And she thought my husband was a diplomat, indeed. As if I were used to gracing odd functions at his side, appeasing natives. As if I couldn't do it on my *own*, she thought, turning on the taps for her bath.

After all, she thought, I did take an interest in them. They were of very great fascination to me. An object lesson. And what else would I have done with my time? I studied them as if they were a subject to which I could apply myself. And having studied them to such an extent I can hardly drop out now. Leave the story before it is finished. But I do think Patrick might have done something. This is much more a job for a man. Whatever they say, it is still a man's world. And if the Demuths are such brutes, surely a man would make more of an impression on them?

She brushed her hair carefully and put on a dress of dark blue linen with a longish skirt. She took a bottle of Sauternes from the fridge and poured a glass, congratulating herself on her mastery of the situation. She would have a serious talk with Patrick and if necessary go with him to the Dorchester. That way conscience would be appeased, honour and dignity saved. The hard blue sky outside the window slowly faded to white, which she supposed was the equivalent of dusk. With her second glass, Blanche quite looked forward to her evening.

Patrick, when he came, wore his habitual grave expression, although his cheeks were slightly, very slightly, flushed. He sat down and refused a glass of wine.

'In a minute, Patrick,' said Blanche, 'I will make you an omelette. A small salad, some bread and butter, and some gooseberry fool. Will that do?'

'This is very good of you, Blanche.'

'It is only an omelette, Patrick.'

'As a matter of fact I am not hungry. Sally gave me a cup of tea and some rather good cake.'

Blanche poured herself another glass. 'It is about Sally that I wanted to talk to you, Patrick. Something must be done.'

'She has told me.'

'Told you?'

'About your very kind offer.'

'My offer?'

'To go and talk to the Demuths.'

Blanche looked at him.

'It is all very irregular, of course. But it might help.'

'Patrick,' said Blanche slowly. 'What I suggested, or what I think I suggested, was that *you* should talk to the Demuths.'

'Oh, no. That is quite out of the question. I could not undertake such a thing in my position. And anyway it would be unwise.'

'Why would it be more unwise for you than for me? Neither of us knows them. They don't know us. They are not going to take up references, you know.'

'I assure you, Blanche, I have discussed the whole thing with my analyst and . . .'

'With your *analyst*?'

'Yes. I go twice a week. She, my analyst, that is, thinks that I must work through my feelings for Sally on my own. Or with her.'

'How very convenient. And what are your feelings for Sally, if I may ask?'

'I wouldn't say this to anyone else, Blanche, but I look on you as an old friend. I am,' he paused significantly, 'emotionally involved.'

'You mean you are in love with her?'

'It is by no means as straightforward as that. Our worlds are very different. And she is a married woman. No, it is more of a . . .' he paused again, 'an emotional attraction.'

'Come to the point, Patrick.'

'It is simply the fact that she belongs to a different world. All the fun she seems to have.' He looked wistful. 'All those parties. I feel she was not made for the harsh realities, such as you and I must face.'

'Life is not a night club, Patrick.'

He took no notice. 'I feel very strongly that what I want to do is to spare her all that. I am, I think, committed to that.'

'But your analyst says that you don't have to do anything about it.'

'Definitely. She is categorical about it. My entire emotional balance is at stake.'

'And mine isn't?'

He looked at her. 'Why should it be? You are merely an observer, an onlooker. I know your ways, you see. You can be quite cold, you know.'

No doubt you have discussed me with your analyst too, thought Blanche. I wonder if your emotional balance was at stake then. On reflection, she thought not.

'And when have you decided that I am to do this deed?' she asked, placing a perfect omelette, crowned with a sprig of parsley, on a tray on his knees.

'Well, they are away this weekend. It seems that Demuth wants to buy a house in the country and Paul is driving them around. But if you were to telephone, perhaps on Monday?'

Blanche laughed. 'I wish I could have an analyst who would stop me doing things like this,' she said. 'Is she very expensive? She sounds as if she is worth every penny you pay her. By the way, what does Sally live on? No, don't answer that. She is like Danae with the shower of gold. Money falls from the sky.'

'This is a very good omelette, Blanche,' said Patrick in a somewhat diminished tone.

Blanche looked at him kindly. 'And am I to report to Sally or to you?'

'To Sally. Of course. My place is in the background.'

'As you wish, Patrick,' said Blanche. 'Coffee?'

N I N E

Suddenly, as it were overnight, the weather became hot and sultry, and Blanche woke each morning in a prickle of heat, the tinny light from the uncurtained window hard on her eyes. These were the dog days, then. With everyone away, or, like Patrick, tactfully absent, she had no incentive to walk about the city, carefully dressed, carefully smiling, and her visits to the National Gallery were suspended. Moving slowly about her drawing-room, Blanche almost wished that it were winter again. With winter you knew where you were: a strict regime could be adhered to, exercise and food could be relied upon to do what they were best at. This summer, so unlike the summers that her memory cherished, was odd, enervating, weighed down by a strident but dusty light that would not go away. Every morning the noise of the last car in the street left an echo which died into emptiness; every evening the air thickened, birds fell silent, and it seemed as if the relieving storm must break. Every morning, when Blanche went out to buy her newspaper, there was an hour of spurious freshness; in the late afternoon, when she went out to buy her ever more desultory dinner, people in the shops would say, 'We need a proper downpour. Clear the air.' But somehow the downpour never came and the air remained uncleared.

Nothing called Blanche from her home. No telephone call disrupted her silence. At times she felt as if she had grown quite wordless, struck dumb by the knowledge of other activities going on elsewhere. As she sat in her dim drawing-room, curtained against the afternoon sun, and surrounded by opened and discarded books, the pictures in her mind took on a brilliance which she supposed was an accurate picture of reality. She thought of the world of holidays, to which others were admitted and from which she now seemed to be disbarred, and she saw everyone she had ever loved haloed with brightness, smiling at her as if in a photograph. 'Why not join us, Blanche?' they seemed to say. 'We are out of reach, of course, and we cannot issue invitations; you will just have to try and imagine us. Everyone is here. We may send you a postcard now and then, and we shall certainly tell you all about it when we return. We shall look different then, tanned, younger than you remember us. We shall be so fit that you will look extremely pale in comparison, paler than you thought you looked. That is how you will feel when we show you our photographs. And what have you been doing with yourself? Anything interesting? Seen anyone? What you need is a holiday. Why don't you plan something? Make an effort?' But the efforts she made, habitually, were incommensurate with the sort of efforts that other people thought she should make. And she was too proud to tell them so.

Somewhere across this busy but emptying city were the Demuths, whom she must reach. For some reason she imagined them as a monstrous couple, overweight and bad tempered, tiresome as children, illogical, suspicious, unattractive, the sort of people one would rather avoid. She imagined them corroded by money yet tight-fisted, balked by their ignorance, raging, finding fault. She saw them as gross capitalists, figures from the Weimar Republic, wearing ill-judged jewellery. Somehow she must persuade them against their will, against their better judgment, and against her own, to retain the services of their unreliable factotum, on whom they obviously depended for whatever civilized graces their money was able to command. Sally, of course, had furnished no information about them other than that they were rich and unfair. That this was a child's view had hardly occurred to Blanche, although she herself had pictured them as more corrupt, more complicated, and above all more antagonistic. Whatever skills she had would be needed to counter their powerful and vindictive arguments, yet she felt herself to be weightless, insubstantial, without sufficient identity to justify herself, let alone anybody else. For several days she postponed her telephone call, until, at last, maddened by her own inactivity, she dialled the number and was put straight through to Mr Demuth's suite. A light pleasant voice, with a faintly synthetic accent, answered: she supposed this to be Paul. She imagined Mr and Mrs Demuth sitting puffily in over-stuffed armchairs while their lithe assistant did anything that involved energy or movement. She made an appointment to see them at six o'clock that evening.

When she emerged from the house, from the shuttered drawing-room in which she felt that she had been sitting for a very long time, the heat was stifling. A yellowish light, not altogether healthy, hovered on the edges of her sight, although she fixed her eyes on the unfamiliar street. After so many days of reclusion the bus stop was an adventure, but the long wait made her feel as if everyone had gone away, and that she and Mr and Mrs Demuth were separated only by a snarl of meaningless and unpopulated traffic. The bus, when it came, was an enormous novelty, and, once seated, she felt her heart beating rather hard. In this unaccustomed heat her clothes felt burdensome. In Knightsbridge, crowds of tourists swirled around Harrods; a pneumatic drill sent out urgent and peremptory messages. This, obviously, was where everyone was. She had forgotten that people were still working. They stood at home-going bus stops with slack and uncomplaining faces, their bags at their feet. Again she envied them, those tired women and girls, for the context in which they lived, for the homes to which they were wearily going. The contrast between her quiet backwater and the noisy centre was strident, overwhelming. She began to look forward to getting back, to her own modest evening ritual which began earlier and earlier these days. Sometimes she went to bed when it was still light. This nervous yellowish glare made her feel threatened, as did the press of traffic in Park Lane. She summoned up her most urbane smile and wished she had had a drink before leaving home.

In the lobby of the Dorchester bowls of stupendous flowers stood in alcoves bathed in artificial light which almost exactly duplicated the quality of the light outside. In the noiseless lift, Blanche began to feel, uneasily, the lack of air. There was a tiny edge of panic in her mind at the idea of all that she must accomplish before she could be safely at home again. I have been too much alone, she thought; it has weakened me. An impulse to turn tail, to flee from this business which, after all, had nothing to do with her, was beginning to mature, but before her hand started to reach for the button that would take the lift down again the door slid open and there stood Paul.

At least, she assumed it was Paul. His smile was sunny, welcoming, and his hand was held out. He was larger than she had expected, taller, sturdier. He was even older. He was, she saw, a man of about thirty-six, handsomely barbered, and kitted out in a pale safari suit. He did not look like anybody's employee. Nor did he look like anybody's husband. He looked entirely temporary, like a stage character. Perhaps it was something to do with the smile, Blanche thought, that radiant smile and that cocked head. He seemed to be in excellent health and entirely unconcerned. But the smile, with its intimation of childish, unprocessed, good nature, and a desire to please unmitigated by any sort of probity, began to worry her, as did the angle of the head, held slightly on one side. It was the angle which Van Gogh had captured in his extremely disturbing portrait of an actor, a man whose very thick hair and eyebrows and strained tilting head convey an impression of madness. But Paul was clearly not mad, or if he was then so was everybody else; it was simply a long time since anyone had smiled at her with such religious eagerness. She noticed, as he turned to open the door of the suite, that he was wearing very expensive shoes.

The sitting-room into which he ushered her was palely opulent, immaculate, upholstered, and decked with more flowers, not quite serious; the resemblance to a stage set and to actors increased, as did her claustrophobia. When Mrs Demuth appeared, with excellent good manners, almost at once, it was as if she too had made an entrance.

'Mrs Vernon?' she asked, in a lilting, little girl's voice. 'Do sit down. My husband is on the telephone. I'm sure he won't be long.'

The immediate impression that Mrs Demuth made was one of pained abstraction and uneasy cosmopolitanism. She was a tall plump woman with a blood-red discontented mouth and wondering eyes. She was dressed in a green silk caftan which brought out greenish lights in her improbably blonde hair, and much gold jewellery. There, at least, Blanche had been right. Everything else about Mrs Demuth confounded her. There was an artlessness about the woman that she had not expected. Mrs Demuth looked in need of protection, as if she were in some subtle way disabled, although her figure was upright and her gaze direct. The artlessness came out in her gold kid sandals, her tiny hands, the aroma of scent and alcohol that her gestures displaced, and the handkerchief with its deep border of lace with which she dabbed her chin from time to time. It was clear to Blanche that this woman, trained to idleness, had been married for her money and humiliated ever since. Like certain people who never forgive their creditors, Mr Demuth had never forgiven his wife for being the only available rich woman capable of tiding him over at a difficult point in his earlier life. She had bored him in proportion to the degree in which his affairs had prospered ever since. Idle and innocent, Mrs Demuth did not appear to understand her unhappiness. Blanche saw her, abandoned by harsher women friends, who only appreciated her husband's company, thoughtfully eating cakes in deserted salons. On her swollen childish wrists her bracelets had a mineral heaviness.

'It is so good of you to come,' she said. She had a faint accent, not quite French, Belgian perhaps. 'Bernard is calling the States. We are going home for six months. Paul, dear, get Mrs Vernon a drink. Will you have some champagne? I always drink it around this time. It is very good for low blood pressure, you know?' Paul, still smiling, moved with boyish alacrity to the ice bucket on a side table and expertly opened a bottle of champagne, the muffled pop heard with evident relief by Mrs Demuth, who dabbed her chin with her handkerchief. 'Is it hot?' she asked. 'We haven't been out today. I get fearfully tired travelling. And London does seem so noisy after Paris.'

'Will Paul be going to America with you?' asked Blanche, accepting a glass of champagne, an inferior drink, she always thought, and one which invariably gave her a headache.

'Oh, I do hope so,' said Mrs Demuth, with evident feeling. She held out her hand, and Paul clasped it, still smiling. 'He is like a son to me, you know. I don't know how I would manage without him.'

It was clear that wealth had rendered her helpless. Her large eyes and sad gestures had a mute and haggard appeal that could only be met by Paul's smiling confidence. She would always, Blanche could see, be uneasy with men of her own age, with their orders and expectations, and would yearn for companionship of a more compliant and sexless nature. She dabbed her chin and handed her glass to Paul, who, still smiling, refilled it. He looked enquiringly at Blanche, whose head had begun to throb: he seemed to invite complicity, as if the two of them might be united in this work of soothing and protecting Mrs Demuth. But that is not what I am here for, thought Blanche, as the headache began its ominous shift into her left eye. At least, I don't think it is.

'I am really longing to get home to the States,' confided Mrs Demuth, who seemed quite uninterested in Blanche's purpose. 'We have a lovely place on Long Island. Do you know it?'

'I once visited there with my husband,' said Blanche, but was interrupted by the entrance of a small but powerfully built man in a light tan suit and smoked glasses.

'Well, Colette,' he said. 'That's settled and I hope you're happy. You sail next week. This was not accomplished without difficulty, I may tell you. They said there was no room, and they expected me to believe them. It has taken me', he glanced at a wafer-thin gold watch, 'exactly twenty-five minutes to get them to change their minds.'

'Why, Bernard, that's wonderful. When do we leave?'

'You leave. I don't. I fly home later, when I have finished here. I can't spare the time, as you should know, for deck games and tea dances.'

'But Bernard ...'

'That's it, Colette. Let's hear no more about it. Good evening,' he nodded to Blanche. 'You must be Mrs Vernon. I'll be with you in a moment. I have one more call to make. Come with me, Paul.'

'Bernard ...' trailed Mrs Demuth helplessly, but he was gone, leaving behind him an impression of violence. Nothing he had said had been out of the way and yet all his remarks had been edged with an apparently motiveless

136

sarcasm. His voice was very faintly accented, American overlaying something more guttural, European. His faultless appearance gave out messages of the most expensive appointments available from several countries. Behind the smoked glasses which hid his eyes Blanche could sense a mind working furiously to keep ahead of everyone else, and the frustration of finding too little opposition. Here was a man not notably gifted for domesticity, since domesticity did not mean the dynasty he had originally envisaged. Unlike his wife, he would accept no substitutes. It was clear that he hated Paul, for the same reason that Mrs Demuth loved him: Paul and Mrs Demuth were recognizably akin, while Bernard Demuth was irreducibly alien. What a life he must have, thought Blanche through her headache, in the fondant atmosphere that Paul and Mrs Demuth had arranged so lovingly for themselves. And yet she did not like him, any more than she liked Paul. Mr Demuth, she knew, was tough, impatient, even cruel. What he most decidedly was not was the gross primitive of her imaginings. She saw now that Paul's function was to take Mrs Demuth off Mr Demuth's hands. In her mind's eye she could see the two of them, window shopping in the Faubourg Saint-Honoré, buying useless articles that Mrs Demuth might not wear. No doubt on these expeditions little presents for Paul or for Sally had been acquired. Who knows if even the red fox coat had been passed on by Mrs Demuth, a gift that was probably disputed by her husband? And money, too, would have been acquired in the same way since Mrs Demuth, resigned, knew from her marital experience that such attentions must be paid for. Was this the answer to the charge of embezzlement, or was embezzlement a kinder word for extortion? The handsome Paul would be a great asset to a lonely and vulnerable woman; as long as he waited on her with the devotion which no son could sustain and no lover would volunteer, he might make his own arrangements in his free time. Yet Blanche saw that Mrs Demuth and Paul were also alike in their apparent, or even their real, sexlessness. Life had frightened them; now they merely desired approval, and were willing to pay for it.

She cleared her throat and sat up a little straighter, since the headache was now threatening the vision in her left eye. 'It was about Paul that I came,' she said firmly. 'I expect you know that his wife and his little daughter miss him very much.' As soon as the words had left her mouth she wondered if they were true. She went on, 'Sally, his wife, gave me to understand that there were certain difficulties, and she so very much hopes that these can be cleared up.' Mrs Demuth dabbed her chin and looked round her for support. 'Financial difficulties,' said Blanche firmly. She could see that it was going to be very difficult to talk about money to Mrs Demuth, who denied all knowledge of it, and equally difficult to talk about it with Mr Demuth, who almost certainly kept accounts down to the last penny.

'It's all too silly,' said Mrs Demuth, who, Blanche now realized, was very slightly drunk. She had probably started earlier in the day. And that might be an additional duty for Paul, to keep an eye on her. 'Paul, darling,' she called. 'Come here and give Mrs Vernon another drink.' Blanche shook her head with some difficulty as Paul reappeared noiselessly and refilled Mrs Demuth's glass. 'I've ordered you a nice little supper,' he said, the first words he had spoken. 'A club sandwich, just like you had last night. We'll have a cosy evening right here.'

'Just the two of us?' she asked anxiously.

'Just the two of us. Bernard has to go out.'

They both seemed infinitely relieved at this prospect. Blanche saw opportunities for sensible discussion melting away. 'If I could just have a word with your husband?' she said. 'Before he goes out?'

'I doubt if there'll be time,' said Paul, placing himself

firmly under Mrs Demuth's wavering protection. 'He has to see someone at seven.'

'Oh, but I should so like to reassure Sally that everything is all right. Is everything all right, Paul?' she asked, desperate to get home before the full force of her headache was unleashed. She had not had such a bad one for some time: the airless room, the acidity of the champagne, the muffled but ceaseless sound of traffic, were building up to a nightmare. She had visions of being as becalmed in this room as she habitually was in Sally's basement.

'Of course, everything's all right,' said Mrs Demuth. And, 'Tell Sally not to worry,' said Paul. Again they clasped hands.

'You can tell Sally that her husband will be home with her next week,' said Mr Demuth, coming back into the room. 'I am going to have to let him go. I can't afford him any more. He has turned out to be a very expensive young man.'

'But Bernard,' wailed Mrs Demuth. 'You know I can't do without him. Especially as you're not coming home with me. How am I going to manage?'

'You will have to manage,' he said. He had obviously said this many times, and had now and then given up. Although in his late sixties, he was clearly a man of vigorous and furious purpose, and his purpose was elsewhere. It was probably to his advantage to have Paul in his household, even if it did cost him a great deal of money. Blanche saw that it was not the money he minded so much as Paul's dishonesty in not acknowledging the situation. He would rather that Paul colluded with him instead of with his wife. As well as being massively irritated by the two of them, he was, as a man of business, insulted that his employee chose to be fully accountable to his wife rather than to himself. That had not been what he had in mind. He had come up against Paul's flavourless affability, his refusal to admit to anything dubious, anything that might alter the appearance of his filial good manners. Paul, like his handwriting, was not only weak but full of euphemisms. This euphemism, of thought as well as of behaviour, had finally got the better of Mr Demuth's hard-headedness.

'But Bernard,' said Mrs Demuth, two tiny tears slowly making their way down her powdery cheeks, her very red mouth a little smeared. This was obviously how all her sentences began. 'Who's going to open the house? Who's going to take care of the luggage?' She did not ask when he would be home, not particularly wanting to know. There were several varieties of absence in play here, Blanche noted. Mr Demuth would be absent from Mrs Demuth. Paul would be absent from Sally. As far as she could see, nobody would experience a serious degree of discomfort. Paul, who must obviously be frightened somewhere beneath his uninflected smile, preferred to leave his life unexamined and no doubt hoped for that large final payment in much the same spirit as he had always hoped for it; in the meantime he would place himself under the guardianship of Mrs Demuth, whose beleaguered state cried out for his continued attentions. Blanche also saw that although Mrs Demuth was in need of Paul she had lost the ability, if she had ever had it, of pleading his or her case. With the awful passive expectancy of the weak she had a good chance of getting her own way, but this might take more time than Blanche had to offer. For her immediate purpose she must do battle with Mr Demuth: behind her, Mrs Demuth, Paul, Sally and Elinor lined up with their demands.

'I don't know how things stand at the moment,' she said cautiously, 'but it looks as if it might be in everyone's interest if Paul stayed on with you for a bit. I'm sure that matters can be regularized without much difficulty. And I know that Sally would be very relieved if they could.'

'I'm not interested,' said Mr Demuth. 'And I doubt if *I*

should be relieved if they could. Pipe down, Colette,' he added, as Mrs Demuth gave a slight moan. 'You're to blame as much as he is. Letting him spend my money. Who do you think he is?'

Blanche saw a serious rage, based on a long-standing grievance, begin to gather like an approaching storm, like the atmospheric storm outside that threatened to break but never did. 'If there's anything I can do to help matters,' she began. 'I mean financially.'

'Why, no, Mrs Vernon, Blanche, don't even think of it,' said Mrs Demuth. 'I may call you Blanche, mayn't I? Paul has told me what a good friend you've been to the family. Don't even think about the money. After all, I have plenty of my own.' She gave her husband a sideways look.

'Well, that's just fine,' he said. 'Because you're going to need every cent of it. He's not getting any more of mine. If you want to hire him, you do. That's the deal from now on. He can take you back home and he can open the house and get you settled in, and that's it. I'll pay his fare back to England, and if he behaves himself he can earn himself a little bonus. But no more from me. No more Paris, no more Cap Ferrat, no more Venice, and above all no more shopping. Is that clear?'

Mrs Demuth reached for Paul's hand. 'Why, Bernard,' she said. 'I don't know what you're getting so upset about.' Now that she had got her way she professed ignorance of the whole affair. Another trait that she and Paul had in common was their love of short-term solutions, based on a genuine inability to look ahead. Sliding away from immediate difficulty was their only concern. It was clear from Paul's very slight degree of relaxation, almost invisible except to a trained eye, that he had not even been seriously worried; clearly, this battle had been fought before. As long as Mrs Demuth controlled her own money the situation could repeat itself indefinitely. And they were all a party to this.

141

Demuth's violence was based not only on his contempt for Paul and for his wife but on his own desire to convert them into responsible people; not only on his inability to get them to think clearly, but even more on his inability to get them to feel anything beyond their own needs. He despaired of them. His wife he had despaired of long ago. Hiring Paul had been one way of dealing with her. Now he despaired of Paul because there was no way of getting rid of him. If he got rid of him he would be saddled with his wife again. Rage fuelled his movements, coloured his expensive beige face. Although ugly, he was in his way an attractive man. Paul, on the other hand, had relaxed into a graceful balletic pose, his hands on the back of Mrs Demuth's chair, his head tilted to one side. Still smiling, he presented a sunny countenance to them all. So thoroughly was he subsumed into Mrs Demuth that he did not even thank Blanche for her errand. No doubt, thought Blanche, that a conspiratorial squeeze of the hand would come her way in due course. Complicity was what was required of her. She made one more effort.

'I believe Sally was worried about her fur coat,' she said, shielding her left eye with her hand.

The more she thought about it the more she could see that Paul would have excellent taste. His feminine sensibility, which, beneath the boyish candour of his appearance, was the essence of his real character, would give him a true appreciation of women's fashions and appointments. It was unlikely that he could satisfy what was probably a very creative appraisal of these matters on Mrs Demuth; only in the smaller consideration of ornaments, jewellery, scarves, would their heads come together in serious consultation. For larger designs, for the desire to create a beautiful appearance in a woman, Paul would use the absent Sally, describing to Mrs Demuth her looks and her style, until Mrs Demuth, fascinated by this essentially feminine chronicle, would unite with him in adding to Sally's wardrobe. The act of giving, of patronage, relieved, and, in some serious way, satisfied them both. It confirmed them in their benevolence. For Mrs Demuth it meant one more demonstration of her desire to please, and – for she thought of herself as lovable – of her ability to do so. For Paul, it affirmed, through multiple zones of doubt, his credentials as a husband. A husband was someone who went out into the world and brought back trophies for his wife. In this matter of the fur coat he had brought back the most primitive trophy of them all.

Blanche, with the acuity of perception habitually conferred on her by her headaches, saw that the fur coat pertained to a moral area even more dubious than any encountered so far, and immediately wished that she had not mentioned it. It was clear, from Paul's abstracted gaze out of the window, from Mrs Demuth's slow and absorbed turning of the bracelets on her wrists, that they had rather the whole matter had been left in the limbo to which they consigned all disagreeable or disputed matters. Paul, with tears in his eyes, might thank Mrs Demuth for giving him the fur coat before she even knew that she had done so, but this would be in one of their intimate tête-à-têtes, and without witnesses. Blanche knew that any understanding she might manage to extract from them would be worthless; nevertheless, she felt it a matter of honour to see the episode through to the end, for once she had fulfilled her obligations down to the last scruple she could collapse into the nirvana of her bed and let the headache take its monstrous three-day toll. During that time she could not afford to have the slightest dissonant thought, for thoughts clanged like bells through her disordered perceptions and must be cancelled as soon as possible.

'The coat?' she repeated, though rather faintly.

'Oh, the coat,' murmured Mrs Demuth, vaguely, as if she could hardly recall which coat they were talking about.

'Don't worry about the coat,' said Paul. 'We'll work something out.' He apparently favoured this phrase as much as Sally did. No doubt they had often reassured each other in this manner, or maybe it was a kind of mantra which enabled them to postpone or even to abandon any decisive action.

'What coat?' asked Mr Demuth, who had reappeared in the doorway unnoticed by any of them. Noiseless, Mr Demuth possessed the power to surprise, to alarm; he could be seen, Blanche thought, to have power over one and was no match for a fainthearted woman. Behind his smoked glasses Mr Demuth seemed embattled, furious with the fates for serving him up this meagre fare, but nevertheless watchful for infringements of his rights. 'If you're talking about that fur you bought in Paris, Colette, that goes straight home with you. You won't want it here.' He gestured through the open window where the sky now showed a sickening yellow.

'Of course, dear,' said Mrs Demuth, making weak affirmative nods. 'Don't worry about a thing. Paul will take care of it.'

Mr Demuth hesitated. 'Goodbye,' he said to Blanche, proffering his hand. 'I hope you'll take back the information you came for.' He seemed to include her in his general contempt, and without seeing the need for further conversation turned and left the room.

'*Well,*' said Mrs Demuth, visibly brightening. 'That's all settled then. Paul, dear, you see Mrs Vernon out. It's been so nice,' she nodded to Blanche. 'And you will give that dear little girl a kiss, won't you. Paul has shown me photographs. And tell Sally she has nothing to worry about. It's all working out.' She made as if to rise to her feet, thought better of it, and sank down again. 'Paul will see you out,' she repeated, looking round. But Paul had already left the room.

In the foyer he was waiting, with the coat over his arm. 'If you could take this with you.' He winked at her. 'With my love,' he added.

'Well, no,' said Blanche. 'I don't think I could.'

'Paul? Paul? Where are you? Has Mrs Vernon gone?' came Mrs Demuth's voice from the salon. Blanche, the warm heavy weight of the coat over her arm, found the door closing on her. Now dizzy, and rather faint, she felt her way to the lift, concentrating very hard on stepping along the corridor without falling. In the lobby, crowded with people making their way to the restaurant and heavy with the intense heat of the approaching storm, she handed the coat to a hall porter. 'Would you take this up to Mrs Demuth's suite?' she asked. 'It was handed to me by mistake.'

T E N

The evening was livid and smelt of drains. To Blanche's disordered senses Park Lane presented a picture of hopeless confusion which she could not begin to disentangle. Cars and buses bore down on her, but not, as far as she could see, a single taxi: there had been none outside the hotel and her anxiety to leave had been so great that she had not thought to wait there. Even now, creeping down the side of the street and clinging to the buildings, she could feel the warm slithering weight of the coat as Paul had thrust it into her arms. Any reaction of outrage was muffled by the fear that in his affectless eagerness he might yet seek her out and pursue her until she was out of sight, convinced that she would, with a little persuasion, perform this minor act of kindness for him. Her hand shielded her left eye as much against Paul as against the gimlet thrusts of the headache. She longed for home with a piercing longing that she had never felt at any other time. That shuttered drawing-room, that cool garden on to which she had projected so many wistful thoughts, comparing it unfavourably with that other garden in her memory, now appeared to her to have the remoteness of a dream, but a dream of order and rightness, a dream to set against the moral sickliness of the adventure for which she had so haplessly volunteered. Inching her way down Park Lane, in the smell of exhaust fumes and under the glare of the unconsummated storm, she forced herself to think ahead to the white bed that awaited her, and saw herself, shriven, in a long robe, waiting by her window, one hand holding back the curtain, for the first drops of rain to fall. I must get home before the storm, she thought, but she saw no means of doing so.

The strangest pictures came to mind. When what she craved was an image of comfort, of succour, of forgiveness, and even – why not? – the face of a compassionate mother, or of any of those obscure saints who seek no martyrdom but are content with their humble destinies, she saw only the nymphs and deities who, apparently, in the world of art, inhabit the same heaven, sailing on clouds that seem to be moving faster when they are not freighted down with human hopes and prayers. In that sky, which is always blue, they sail, impervious to mortal needs, above the world of just deserts, leaving on earth the pilgrims seeking their glimpse of salvation. Forever in motion, as if buoyed on the thermals rising from the aspirations of the unenlightened, inscrutable, weightless. And the gods, striding with all their ideal muscularity into new liaisons, or smiting, wrestling, rising, setting, identifying with the cosmos of which they are embodiments, and bearing in their faces the ardour of the beginning of the world. Not, then, the confusion of Adam and Eve, mawkishly, stupidly, ashamed, half-heartedly instinctive, and instantly, massively, rebuked, but the plunderers, the conscienceless, the plausible, scattering their children, seeking their pleasure, vanquishing their rivals, and, always, moving on. She saw no clear message here, only a huge, a gigantic conflict of principle, a conflict which engages the attention of the entire human race but which is rationalized in terms of lesser mythologies. Looking up with difficulty, she saw the lumbering shuddering buses, panting like animals at traffic lights, the humble trudge of the army of homegoers, the glaring wretched light. As she reached the extreme edge of the pavement, at Hyde Park Corner, she stopped, knowing that she could go no further. She must stay here, if necessary until darkness fell, until the street became empty; she must endure until help, in the shape of a taxi, came to take her away.

Distant thunder rumbled. In the garden, Adam and Eve seem strangely unconscious of the wonders of creation but slyly preoccupied with their lower natures. Blanche saw that all acts committed in that state of mind are shameful; energy and bliss are needed to transform them into the laws of life. Maybe that was the lesson, she told herself, feeling that she was on the verge of some great discovery, though too tired to understand it. She saw too that energy and bliss exonerate but do not provide conclusions; they are the motive power which must, somehow, be captured, harnessed. The desire for a resting place is the unavoidable constraint. She had once thought of herself as such a resting place, and had indeed rested there. But beyond her resting place was the lure, the excitation of inexhaustible movement, of endless possibility, of becoming, of transformation. As she leant carefully on a railing which separated her from the still-vast concourse of traffic, with her left eye closed, and sometimes, in an access of faintness, her right eye as well, Blanche thought of mournful Adam and Eve, enactments of the fallen creation, but also of the sometimes squalid stratagems of the gods, merciless predators, cunning manipulators, thoughtless progenitors, proponents of greater though at the same time lesser misdemeanours. To a sceptical eye, to an eye so enlightened as to have gazed on the highest wisdom, the Beamish family might, to a certain extent, be termed mythic. But if the alternative was to wait anxiously for a sign of forgiveness, whose principles could be said to be more questionable?

She saw too that her business with the Beamishes was at an end, that in fact they no longer required her, that her presence might cloud their faces with boredom; by her very acts she had made herself redundant. The little girl was consigned, sadly, to the careless whims of her parents. Yet the sadness too was perhaps redundant or merely out of place; Elinor had been sprung on the world in puzzling, even daunting circumstances and was already strong enough to choose her own destiny. In time the parents would cease to be important, would fall away, like exploded stars, or, more simply, move on. The world belonged to the young, to the cunning, to the obdurate. Blanche, under the threatening sky, spared a thought for Elinor and wished for her qualities of mythological dimensions and consistency. As to that dubious charade at which she had assisted earlier that evening, was that not a demonstration of declining powers, of the advance of corruption, of vanishing effectiveness? Was it not a sign that Elinor would need all her qualities to be stronger and more merciless than the circumstances which had brought her to birth?

For Blanche saw that there was something strangely restricting about the life of eternal freedom, as manifested by Paul and Sally, and that the ageing soul, not to speak of the ageing body, requires and deserves its resting place. She saw too that time misspent in youth is sometimes all the freedom one ever has; that is why the gods are always young. Except for Jupiter, thought Blanche; but his is the example to confound all the others. For the rest, it is enough to become stars, petrified yet luminous, and with the power to guide mariners. It would perhaps be fitting for Paul and Sally to fall away from mortal sight, as they no doubt planned to do in some discreet and untraceable way, and merely leave as a legacy to their daughter an after-image of smiling carelessness. At this prevision of the heedless continuum of certain forms of behaviour, Blanche shivered in the prickly damp heat; somewhere above her left eye she saw the blind fixity of the archaic smile. She waited for a sign of grace, a sign to displace her worst imaginings, but no sign came.

Time passed. It was perhaps an hour since she had left the hotel, perhaps an hour and a half. The yellow sky darkened; very occasionally thick drops of rain fell and then stopped. The heated ground drank up the moisture immediately, but from the park came an occasional breath of damp air. In her strange and almost illuminated state of mind, in the airy insubstantiality sometimes conferred by extreme pain, Blanche rested and let her head sink down upon her railing. No one seemed to find this extraordinary; there was enough madness about to absorb her aberrant appearance and behaviour. The sight of a woman impeccably dressed yet apparently gazing with fascination at the vibrating side of a Number 36 bus and intermittently bowing her head in prayer caused no ripples of consternation. No one paused in concern or hurried by with averted face; no one hurried at all, but merely passed by in a trance of concentration. Freed by this evidence of the existence of other worlds, of the continued dance of the atoms regardless of her own passivity, Blanche rested her exhausted consciousness. When she could bear to open both eyes she saw merely a darkening sky, and on the other side of the great street a racing stream of traffic anxious to flee the storm.

The taxi, when it came, seemed as exhausted as she herself was; shuddering, it drew up at the railing around which she gracelessly sidled. In the aromatic interior of the cab, its overflowing ashtrays vying with a powerful deodorant, her faintness returned, and her hand crept to her throat as she painfully counted the minutes that separated her from the haven of her home. She was unable, now, to turn her head. Darkness filled the air; it was perhaps nine o'clock. The extreme tension of the atmosphere detonated outbreaks of anxiety in the driver; swerving, he muttered to himself and occasionally punched the wheel with his fist. She was lucky, he told her; he was going home to Putney, turning it in for the night. This was no night to be out. All right, are you?

he called back to her. Thought you looked a bit funny.
Wouldn't have stopped otherwise. Get you home soon, he
said, leaning on the horn. With an enormous effort Blanche
opened her mouth. How kind, she said. Tears coursed from
her right eye.

In her quiet street, now quite dark, windows shone a
golden yellow. Very slowly, her hand supporting her head,
Blanche got out of the cab, proffered notes in a nerveless
hand, and turned to negotiate the steps of her building.
Heavy drops once more fell, hissing on the pavement; a
gritty wind had sprung up. 'Mrs Vernon?' said a voice. 'Mrs
Vernon? Are you all right?' Turning, with infinite caution,
Blanche saw Mrs Duff with some kind of whitish signal in
her hand. 'Are you all right? My husband left his newspaper
in the car and I came out to get it. I wouldn't have bothered
you but you seemed a little strange. Is anything wrong?'
Mrs Duff peered anxiously into Blanche's face. 'Migraine,'
whispered Blanche. A hand came out. 'Lean on me, dear.
Let me find your key. Never mind, dear. Never mind.
You're home now.'

Blanche surrendered to the eternal commiseration of Mrs
Duff, whose sure hand guided her into the stifling stillness
of her bedroom, guided her to the bed, and then opened a
window on to the rising wind and the random scatterings
of the rain. She felt her shoes being removed and a cool
damp cloth applied to her forehead. Then there was an
absence, during which she knew nothing, a little faintness,
a little sleep, perhaps. She was next aware of a whispered
conversation: Mrs Duff had returned with her husband, the
dentist, from whose side she never strayed for long. A dark
silk handkerchief – the dentist's contribution – was placed
over the bedside lamp, and somewhere a kettle was being
filled. Then, in the greenish glow of her shaded lamp, she
saw Mrs Duff's face, calm and beautiful with concern. A
thin fresh herbal smell filled her nostrils, and a cup was lifted

to her lips. 'Drink this,' said Mrs Duff. Then, some time later, she said, 'You'll sleep now.' And then, 'I'll look in in the morning. I'll take your key.' 'Come, Philly,' she heard the husband say. 'She'll sleep now.'

But she did not sleep. She drifted in and out of consciousness as if she were moving slowly down a dark passage. Past her glided the kouroi with their blind fixed smile. At some point she managed to get up, to undress, and to put on her nightgown. Then she sank back on to the pillows with her hands tightly clasped, as if in prayer. Sometimes she thought she saw lightning, but could not be sure if it were outside the window or in her head. She was aware of the darkness of the garden, its heavy leafage stirred by the wind, tiny rustlings, the bell round the neck of the stalking cat. At some point she found that she could open and close both her eyes. She lay in a trance of gratitude for her recovered sight, and the kouroi dissolved, taking with them their eternal smile. Once again she got up and felt her way to the window; her face met coolness, night sounds, the order of the universe restored. Sleep remained far off but she did not mind. This night had been given her; she cherished and praised every moment. Some time at around dawn, when the sky began to pale to a whitish grey, she relinquished her hold on her consciousness. At about five o'clock she slept.

When she awoke, it was to an instant of brilliant well-being. Then the dull throbbing started, and she knew that she was in the second phase of her headache. But this was now manageable; she had reached safety. She would simply have to last out the day until the second night, when, she knew from experience, she would sleep heavily. Already she mildly regretted her sleepless night, although she was still stirred by the strange insights that had preceded it. She resigned herself to a day in bed, and looked forward, with childlike trust, to Mrs Duff's morning visit. There were pills to be taken, ordinary satisfying measures with which to outwit the pain. She thought, like someone who has been ill for a very long time, of the moment of her first bath, of a change of nightgown. The awful evening had left her calm, purged of all imagined obligations. She saw in Mrs Duff's actions the necessary simplicity of all service, and in her own life of the past few weeks a succession of follies, the origin of which she preferred, for the moment, to leave unexamined.

There was the sound of a key in the lock, cautious steps, the kettle being once more filled. Her door opened slowly, to reveal Mrs Duff, efficient in navy blue, having clothed herself in quasi-medical severity. They smiled at each other. 'I can never thank you ...' Blanche began. 'Thank me? Thank me?' bridled Mrs Duff. 'If I can't be a good neighbour, and', she blushed at this point, 'a friend, I should like to know what I'm worth.' 'A very good friend,' said Blanche. Mrs Duff beamed with pleasure. 'Could you drink a cup of tea?' she asked. 'And is there anything you should take?' 'My pills are on the dressing-table,' said Blanche. 'And do come in and have a cup with me.'

This invitation broke Mrs Duff's hitherto heroic silence, but there is always a price to be paid, as Blanche knew well. During the next hour she heard a great deal about Mrs Duff's husband's likes and dislikes, her plans for a winter holiday in the Canary Islands ('although he does hate to go away; I have to bully him'), her sister in Oxford who had suffered from migraines as a girl but had grown out of them ('and I never knew what a headache was; aren't I lucky?'), her plans to redecorate her bedroom ('of course, I shall do it all myself'), and her life at home with Mother, who had, surprisingly, been a designer of hats and a court milliner. These revelations had the charm of a fairy tale for Blanche, and although her head ached, she gazed with fascination at Mrs Duff's fine arched brows, her slightly protuberant blue eyes, and her mobile mouth, the corners of which turned down in unconscious melancholy whenever she stopped talking. Of course, Blanche remembered, there was the little baby who had never come along, no matter how devoted a couple Mrs Duff and her husband were and had always been. This subject was clearly never far from Mrs Duff's mind. Presently her eyes filled with tears. 'I saw you with that little girl,' she said. 'For one lovely moment I thought all was well again. You know what I mean. You haven't been very happy, have you?' She dabbed her eyes. 'You must forgive me,' she said. 'Some things you never get over, do you?' She sighed. 'But this won't do. You're the one who needs cheering up. Is there anyone you want me to get in touch with?' 'No,' said Blanche, closing her eyes and feeling suddenly tired. 'Everyone is away.'

Persuading Mrs Duff to leave and go about her normal day's concerns was no easy task but it was somehow and at length accomplished. Promising to look in again that evening, Mrs Duff pocketed Blanche's key, picked up her smart straw bag, and left. Alone, Blanche lay back thankfully, but again sleep did not come. It seemed, however, as if Mrs Duff's reminiscences had banished the antique demons from her interior vision, leaving behind a wistfulness, a desire to have the horizon filled with other figures. A desire also came to her for an impeccable conscience. If I had been a wife like Mrs Duff, she thought, Bertie and I could have lived as one; instead, I sloped off by myself, and through shyness became quaint. I was not a comfortable person to be with, although I may have been an interesting one. Turning her eyes to the window, she saw drifting veils of rain, for the storm had not broken but had merely retired somewhere else. Weeping skies, and the heavy dark foliage of late summer, made the air in the room seem dense, unmoving. Yet the temperature had noticeably dropped; perhaps the season had ended. The darkness that had filled her vision the night before had perhaps been the true darkness of night falling, rather than the fading vision brought about by her headache. '*Je redoute l'hiver parce que c'est la saison du confort,*' thought Blanche, and comforted herself with pictures of Mrs Duff as a little girl, playing with her mother's hats, being cosseted by the girls in the workroom, entranced by the women who came for fittings. For she has that intense femininity that comes from growing up in a woman's world, thought Blanche: a world of confidences, secrets, remedies shared. And it has kept her innocent. She knows nothing of the suspect side of femininity, its conspiratorial aspects, its politics. I am sure that she has never engaged in the sizing up of another woman's chances that disfigures so much female thinking; and I am quite sure she has never done that nasty thing, pretended to be sorry for her women friends in the presence of a man. I am sure that she has never needed to mention another woman to her husband, slyly, to gauge his reaction, because, quite clearly, she is the only woman for him. Philly, he called her. Little Philly, trying on the grown-ups' hats. He probably inherited the name from her mother, and so an unbroken chain of affection has nourished her all through her life. I should like to have been a little girl myself; it might have given me more winning ways. But there was always Mother, waiting for me to grow up and take charge, reminding me of onerous duties. Do it now!

Well, I did it, she thought tiredly, and this is where I am. And my conscience is still not clear.

The rest of the day passed slowly and silently. The rain settled down to a steady drizzle, and she heard it pattering on the leaves. At about five o'clock she got up, her eyes weak and smarting, one hand automatically shielding her head. Cautiously she bathed and changed, then got back, shivering, into bed. She reckoned that this might take another day; then she would accord herself the luxury of a day's convalescence. She began to look forward to Mrs

Duff's next visit. Giving Mrs Duff the key had made her feel trustful, like a child who can expect to be cared for. She even looked forward to the dark, to the drawing of the curtains and the lighting of her lamp, still shrouded in Mr Duff's green silk handkerchief. When the telephone rang, she was quite surprised; she had not expected to hear from anyone. The bubble of illness in which she was enclosed had seemed to preclude conversations with the outside world. Her pain had required her entire concentration. For all practical purposes she was absent.

'Blanche?'

'Barbara! When did you get back?'

'This afternoon. My dear, the weather was so awful that we began to hate every minute of it. And then that terrible storm last night. That started Jack's foot off again, so we thought we'd get back in case it got any worse. Are you all right? Your voice sounded a bit odd.'

'A headache. I'll be all right in a day or two.'

'Oh dear, I am sorry. You haven't had one for some time, have you? Since that business with Bertie.' There was a silence. 'Perhaps you ought to lie down for a bit. Shall I look in tomorrow. Do you need any shopping?'

'Actually, I'm in bed. And I haven't got a spare key. My very kind neighbour took mine. I'll be perfectly all right in a day or two. It's lovely to talk to you, but I won't talk any more just now, if you don't mind. My voice sounds like a gun to me.'

'My dear girl! Thank goodness I came back. I'll ring tomorrow. If there's anything you need ...'

'Nothing, thank you. So glad you're back. Love to Jack.'

Lights went on in the corridor; Mrs Duff had returned. She had changed into a striped silk dress; she probably changed every evening, smartening herself up for her husband's return. She came in, beaming, important, with another cup of tea and some strips of dry toast spread with bitter marmalade, and stood by while Blanche made an effort to eat. When the telephone rang again, Mrs Duff darted to answer it, listened for a moment, and then said, impressively, 'Mrs Vernon is unwell. Who shall I say called?'

'A Mr Fox,' she remarked to Blanche. 'He sounded agitated. He would like you to call him back.'

He might like me to, thought Blanche, but I don't think I will. If he is agitated he can ring his analyst. The person I should ring, of course, is Sally. The thought of Sally brought with it an onslaught of exhaustion. When I'm stronger, she promised herself. When I have decided what to say. For although she remembered every word of the interview at the hotel she had not quite got round to summing it all up. There was unfinished business here, and she did not know how to finish it.

Mrs Duff placed a jug of lemon barley water by her bed. 'My husband swears by it. I make it myself, of course. And I've left a cold chicken in the fridge and a fruit salad. I dare say you'll be quite hungry by tomorrow. Now is there anything else you want this evening?'

For Mrs Duff, Blanche could see, was anxious to go next door and cook her husband's dinner: older loyalties prevailed. When she had left, the silence was complete. Darkness had fallen early; the miserable day was over. Leaves dripped outside in the garden. The headache had settled down to a heaviness in the eyes and a sensitivity in the skin of the face and the head; she would be unable to brush her hair for another night. Lying in bed was all that she was required to do, but now she felt less comfortable about it. The sadness of childhood recalled, and the greater sadness that had come with her middle age, turned her thoughts to melancholy and the desire for consolation. In this situation, and unwatched, her brisk mannerisms were of no use to her. They had been summoned up for the benefit of others, of course, and fuelled by the wrong sort of pride. She knew now that real pride means gusto; real pride involves fearlessness, bravado, confidence, not a façade behind which one cowers, perplexed, like Adam and Eve in their wretched dilemma, eternal children with a problematic parent they were too inexperienced to challenge. She felt exhausted by the sheer continuity of it all. Wrong start, wrong finish. It was, in fact, characters like Sally and like Mousie who had pride, who went into the jungle of human affairs with nothing but their own weapons to defend them, whereas Paul, now that she came to think of it, had exactly the unthinking placatory attitude that doomed him in his quest for strength. Paul, to a certain extent, was Adam. His trouble was that he had got mixed up in the wrong mythology. Sally (whom she must telephone) would go on to other partners: Paul would be stuck with Mrs Demuth, with Mr Demuth always at hand to castigate him. It was a situation which could not be resolved.

And I must stop making stories out of these people, creating false analogies, reifying and mythologizing them, she thought. I have let the National Gallery go to my head. It was this sort of thing that drove Bertie mad.

When she felt stronger (and at the thought she immediately felt weaker) she would telephone Sally, and simply report what had happened. There seemed to be little more that she could do. She might leave another contribution or two under the lid of the teapot, but since she suspected that funds came from elsewhere, she would not make a habit of it. Perhaps Sally would have to be sent off to America to join Paul: this was a very expensive possibility, and yet there seemed no way of escaping from the coils of this dilemma except by extreme actions, such as providing two airline tickets. Surely she was not to be involved to this extent? And yet it seemed likely. It even seemed likely that her conscience was not to be appeased by anything less. Perhaps Patrick might have a better idea, although, knowing Patrick, it would be an idea that favoured non-intervention. Possibly, at this very moment, Patrick was proceeding from Sally to his analyst, or vice versa. The little girl, who had never spoken in Blanche's presence, and who was reputed never to speak at all, was the one to be saved. But Blanche once again saw that she had identified too closely with Elinor, and that Elinor might yet learn those lessons that she, Blanche, had never mastered.

Cautiously lifting her head, she addressed herself to the telephone and dialled Patrick's number. He answered at once, as if he had been waiting for the call.

'Patrick?' she said, in a voice which sounded to her three tones higher than normal. 'It's Blanche. I'm afraid I'm not very well. I won't talk long, if you don't mind.' The telephone hummed with excited silence.

'What news?' asked Patrick, after a short interval, as if he had given her quite enough time to recover.

'Well, I don't really know. I saw those people and they're really quite ordinary, quite respectable. But it's a funny set-up. I think they're keeping Paul on for a bit, taking him back to America. The whole thing is really out of my hands. It was never really in my hands, as you know. I shall certainly not pursue it further.'

'I see,' said Patrick heavily.

'I'll telephone Sally, of course, when I feel a bit better. And then I think it's over to you, if you think you can help. But I would somehow advise against it. Oh, let me talk to you tomorrow or the day after, when I'm myself again. I'm afraid I can't say any more just now.'

'I'm in your debt, Blanche,' said Patrick, in the same heavy tone. 'I have come to a few decisions myself. I will talk with you shortly.'

'Goodnight, Patrick,' said Blanche, and thankfully put the telephone down.

Outside the windows a prematurely black night had established itself. After her conversation with Patrick, the silence was so total that Blanche stirred deliberately in the bed to find out if she could hear herself. It was just as well, she thought, that she was not an hysterical woman. When she heard the key in the lock she could have clasped her hands in a prayer of gratitude. Mrs Duff had come back, like the Good Samaritan that she was, to say goodnight. But when the door opened, it was to reveal Miss Elphinstone, in her navy blue coat, a plastic rain hood tied loosely over her hat, and bringing in with her her usual air of ecclesiastical gentility.

'Good evening, Blanche,' said Miss Elphinstone. 'I was visiting at the hospital, so I thought I'd look in on my way home and see how you were getting on. Terrible weather we had, and not much better here, I see. Black as Egypt's night outside.' And she stepped briskly to the window and pulled the curtains. Immediately the room seemed manageable. Blanche sat up in bed and removed the silk handkerchief from the lamp. 'Shall we have a cup of tea?' she suggested. 'It's good to see you.'

'Well, yes, I could do with a cup,' said Miss Elphinstone judiciously, and went to put the kettle on.

'Well, you look as if you could do with a break and no mistake,' she continued as she came back with the tray. 'In bed at nine o'clock. And that nice chicken in the fridge not touched. Not one of our dishes, by the way.'

'I've had a bad headache,' said Blanche. 'I should be all right by tomorrow. You know how these things go. Mrs Duff brought the chicken. She's been so kind.'

Miss Elphinstone pursed her lips and drank her tea thoughtfully. 'I'll look in tomorrow and give you a hand,' she said. 'No need to get up if you don't feel like it. You'll want to eat something before you go out on manoeuvres again. Just as well I'm back, isn't it?

'This will interest you, Blanche,' she went on, removing something from her leather hold-all and handing it to

Blanche. It was a colour photograph, slightly out of focus, of about eight or ten women, those on the edges of the print indicated by little more than an elbow. 'Taken outside the Bird Sanctuary at Bourton-on-the-Water. That's the Women's Fellowship. Of course, if a certain person had stepped back a bit we could all have got in. I'm naming no names,' she said firmly. 'But what an opportunity wasted. After that the camera got mislaid. But that's another story.'

'It's very good of you,' said Blanche sincerely, for Miss Elphinstone was conspicuous in the middle of the group, leather hold-all well in evidence, worldly smile enhanced by the tilt of an important straw hat. 'You make all the others look frumpish.' For there was something heroic as well as elegant about Miss Elphinstone's demeanour: she could have run a mission station in southern India if she had put her mind to it. She belonged to the days of Empire. She could save a person's life simply by appearing, as she had just now, in the doorway.

'I should say it was a success *on the whole*,' said Miss Elphinstone, retrieving the photograph and giving it a critical glance before putting it away. 'But the weather didn't favour us. And the accommodation wasn't all that commodious. I dare say we shall go back to Devizes next year. And what have you been doing with yourself?'

'Nothing much,' said Blanche, sinking back luxuriously into her pillows. 'Nothing to speak of. It will be nice to get back to normal.' She realized that her notions of normality had become seriously eroded. It was time to get herself back on to a serious footing, whatever that might entail. The alternative was to drift, and that was not to be thought of. It seems that there is still more work to be done, she thought. But sleep was now stealing on her; through half-closed lids she saw Miss Elphinstone's hatted shape standing motionless by the door. And then she thought Miss Elphinstone disappeared, but by this time her eyes were quite shut.

E L E V E N

Bathed and dressed, Blanche took down from her shelves the *Philebus* of Plato and read that the life of pleasure must be mixed with reason and the life of reason must be mixed with pleasure but that a third quality, to which both reason and pleasure look forward, must be the final ingredient of the good life. Realizing, with a slightly sinking heart, that given the choice she might have settled for a life of pleasure, she laid the book aside. Mention of the life of pleasure led her thoughts ineluctably to Sally. She dialled Sally's number, heard the receiver being lifted, heard then a quantity of silence, after which the receiver was replaced. This had now happened a number of times. Elinor, she supposed, picking up the telephone and refusing to answer it. There was nothing for it; she would have to go round there. The idea was not encouraging. I am not really up to this, she thought, as she prepared to leave the flat for the first time since the interview with Mr and Mrs Demuth at the Dorchester. But she felt extraordinarily well, as she usually did after a headache, and the weather was cool and gusty, and she longed for a change of scene. Patrick, agitated but cautious, and portentous with information withheld, had told her nothing. Yet she imagined that Sally, with her preternaturally attuned instincts, had somehow got wind of the situation and barely needed Blanche's confirmation. Nevertheless, she turned her steps to the river and to Sally's basement, where, she thought, the life of reason had barely impinged on the life of pleasure, showing that Sally was in a happier and more primitive state than that envisaged for any length of time by Socrates and his friends.

This time she went empty-handed, except for another book for Elinor. This time, she determined, there would be a final accounting. She felt vigorous and energetic, full of rough good sense, slightly brutal. The onset of the autumn winds had delivered her from the languors of summer. Peering down into the basement from the street, through the dusty windows, she saw several garments abandoned on the sofa that served as a bed, but no other signs of habitation. Ringing the bell brought no answer. Propping Elinor's book up against the door frame, she retraced her steps, slightly disappointed. They must be out shopping, she thought, or possibly at the hospital. Having nothing else to do, she walked up to the hospital and looked round the Outpatients' Department. No sign. Walking back to the flat she wondered idly if Patrick were religious – men of his anxious type often were – and whether he saw the salvation of Sally as some kind of ethical duty. Plato had implied that honour was the essential quality of the good life and that both pleasure and reason led one to a desire for it. She then wondered whether honour were compatible with mixed motives. It was by no means clear.

She made a few desultory purchases, lingering in the sunny street. Back in the flat she cut up the chicken, immersed the pieces in a herby aspic, and made an apple tart. She tried Sally's number once more but there was no reply. Thoughtfully, she telephoned Patrick's office. 'Patrick,' she said. 'I wonder if you could look in this evening? I could give you a light supper. I'm afraid it must be this evening because I am going away. You could? Excellent. About seven?'

She had not thought that she was going away until she had said so. But why not? It was obvious. She was as entitled

163

to a holiday as everybody else, and September was a beautiful month, October an even better one. In the south the autumn sunshine would be lying heavy and golden; the crowds would have emptied away, the children would be back at school. She would go over the Alps to Italy; she would go to Munich and Vienna and sit in the public gardens; she would go to Paris and walk in the park at Versailles. Meditatively, she got out the Continental timetables. A variety of possibilities suddenly seemed to present themselves to her, and she studied the book for the rest of the afternoon. Gradually the pictures in her mind sharpened. She saw the park at Versailles, always deserted in its farthest reaches, golden leaves settled in drifts around the bases of the statues, the water in the stone basins still, undisturbed by the fountains, and mirroring the slow clouds in their lofty movements. She would go to Paris and eat Berthillon's ices, read all the latest books sitting at outdoor cafés, dine early and alone, and sleep a long healing sleep. And then, she thought, shutting the book, of course I shall go south again. Of course. And if I sit alone under the palm trees when everyone is having a siesta, and if there is no one to hurry back for, what of it? The sun is God.

'Patrick,' she said, as she poured out a couple of glasses of Piesporter. 'Have you any idea what you are going to do about Sally? You look very unhappy for a man who is emotionally involved. But then I suppose one often does.'

'Well, actually, I thought of taking her away on a holiday,' he said uncomfortably.

'What a good idea,' said Blanche, in what she hoped was a calm tone. 'I hope you are prepared to spend a great deal of money.' He looked shocked. 'Well, I would hardly imagine that you thought of taking her to the Lake District. I don't know what your usual holidays are like but I imagine them as rather Spartan. Wayside inns, ploughman's lunches; that sort of thing. That will hardly do for Sally. Elinor, of course, will be parked with her grandmother again. Where were you thinking of going?' she asked politely, after a silence containing volumes of unanswered questions.

'I thought of Marbella,' he replied, uneasily. 'Or Ischia.'

'And what will you do there, Patrick? It is hardly your scene, as they say.'

'Whatever Sally wants to do.' He looked increasingly unhappy.

'Patrick,' Blanche said gently. 'Is this honourable? Always remembering that honour is the highest good. Pleasure unmixed with reason is apparently what the unenlightened go in for. It does not guarantee a good conscience.'

'I have had too much of a good conscience,' he remonstrated. 'I work hard. I have no debts. For years I danced attendance on my widowed mother.'

'I thought you were devoted to her.'

'Nevertheless, she required my presence long past the time of my requiring hers. I suppose that is one form of honour.'

'Not really,' said Blanche. 'That is duty. We cannot always choose our duties.'

'We are told to honour our father and mother.'

'I am never sure how far one is expected to go along that line. Most of the parents in the Bible would have been impossible. I notice that we don't hear too much from Job's daughters. What a life they must have had. Besides, the messages in the Bible are by no means clear. Some of them are downright subversive. Remember Uriah the Hittite. What else have you done that puts you in good standing, as Sally would say?'

'I don't suppose I have done much by your standards, Blanche. You were always flippant. I have been ... concerned. Aware. I have not, I think, been unkind.'

'That sentence contains two negatives. Have you been kind, that is the main thing. And, yes, I suppose you have. And there is no reason why I should appear to sit in judgment on you. I am not judging you, Patrick. I simply recognize what you are doing. I have seen it before. Your position is secure. You are respected at work. Your income is stable. You have done your duty. You have honoured your mother and no doubt many other people. Now you want to be reprehensible. You want to commit questionable actions. You want to raise scandalized comment. You want the sheer – what is the word? – exhilaration of it. You want to be free of all your standards and of everybody else's too. And you are right, of course. Whether what you are *doing* is right or not is another matter. You want your own life back. You want autonomy.'

'You understand me well, Blanche.'

'What I don't understand is why men do these things for some women and not for others. Perhaps you can tell me.'

'It is simply that some women make one restless. Others one knows will always be there to come home to. It is as simple as that.'

'No, it is not simple, not if you are one of those other women. When you see men driven to folly, you think, why can't I do that? Not that you want to be a wrecker. But it is never quite clear how far you can go. Perhaps you are waiting to see how far others will be prepared to go. But perhaps you don't wait long enough. Perhaps you don't dare. Perhaps you don't even like waiting. Perhaps you want to rush in with your own contribution: wanting to make things quicker and easier all round.'

'But I think Sally has done all that.'

'Well, no, I don't think she has. Sally, as far as I can see, has made no contribution at all.'

'Sally is her own contribution.'

'Ah yes, I see. How sad it all is.'

'Sad?'

'Well, yes, I think it is rather sad. For you, not necessarily

166

for her. You forget that the Sallies of this world are very good at discarding.'

'But that is the way of the world, Blanche.'

'To discard? To lighten the load? Is it?'

'If you want your own way, it is.'

'You mean that nature tells us to look after number one? And all the rest is superstructure, ethical systems perpetrated on us by old men?'

'In a way.'

'But if that were so nature would tell us to desert our parents when they became tiresome, murder our rivals, take what we wanted, no matter how much it cost other people.'

'Nature simply tells us to enjoy ourselves from time to time.'

'I know that, Patrick. And perhaps you are willing to pay the price.'

'What is the price?'

'Ah, nobody knows. That is the catch, you see.'

'I think I am willing to pay it.'

'Then you had better telephone Sally, while I mix the salad. For some reason she doesn't answer.'

'I will ring her later, Blanche. When I get home.' He assumed the faraway look of one who will shortly communicate with the Muses. Clearly he telephoned her every night, deriving emotional sustenance from her vague and elliptical remarks, marvelling at the sheer unfamiliarity of it all, and believing that unaccountability contains erotic messages, messages of intrigue, of favours withheld, of penalties meted out. Delighting in the danger.

'I have thought that I might arrange for Elinor to have a little money,' said Blanche, coming back with the tray. 'When she is seventeen. That is the age at which to commit follies. Of course, I would rather not. The money wouldn't matter, but I have a feeling that I am buying off my conscience and doing a very dreary thing at the same time. It is

167

what old ladies do, always postponing things as long as they can. And who is to say that Elinor will not turn out like her parents?'

'Sally is actually quite a good mother.'

'Yes, I can see that she might be great fun. But I have the feeling that Elinor does not quite like all this fun. She is a much more serious person.'

'She is only three years old, Blanche. We don't know what she will become.'

'No, and I don't intend to wait and see. She is not my child and nothing could ever make her so. I have never wanted substitutes. Or I don't think I have. When I first saw her, I thought she looked lonely. I know about lonely children. Some people are lonely children all their lives. I think I wanted to prevent that. As far as that goes, I suppose I too was emotionally involved.'

'I have often wondered why you had no children of your own.'

'So have I.' She looked down. 'Do have some more of this chicken, Patrick. A kind neighbour brought it when I was unwell.' She noticed that he had not asked after her, admittedly restored, health. He is far gone, she thought. But then it was the intensity of his self-absorption that had always stood in the way of greater intimacy. Until this evening, when they seemed to be speaking naturally, she had always had the feeling that he counted any personal remark she made as a kind of intrusion on his own stream of consciousness. He is not only far gone, she thought: he has gone as far as he is likely to go. When they no longer have the telephone to keep them apart but are forced into daily contact, they will reveal themselves to each other. And then she saw that this was all a dream of Patrick's, that Sally would never go away with him, not even to Marbella or to Ischia. Sally's instincts were too good. She saw the self-absorption, the undeniable respectability, the wistful desire to regress; above all, she saw

168

the sheer lack of practice. Sally saw all this; that was why she was currently unavailable.

The sound of a key in the lock brought her back to her own circumstances, and she prepared herself to entertain Patrick and Mrs Duff for the rest of the evening. But it was Bertie who stood in the doorway, looking tanned and annoyed.

'I thought you were ill,' he said. 'Barbara said you were ill. Good evening, Patrick.'

'Patrick looked in to see how I was,' said Blanche smoothly, feeling a trifle faint. 'I will sit down for a moment, if you don't mind. I think I have been quite unwell.'

'Not too unwell to cook, I see,' said Bertie, eyeing the apple tart. After a minute or two he helped himself to a slice. Nobody said anything. He ate moodily, distancing himself from enjoyment, as one does in the presence of the sick.

'And how was Crete?' asked Blanche.

'Corfu. Very hot. Rather noisy. There seemed to be a number of people there one knew. Or almost knew. You know how it is. Dinner with a crowd of about ten every night. Great fun, of course. Enormously enjoyable.'

'How was the villa?' asked Blanche, thinking of dinner with a crowd of about ten every night.

'Well, we shared it with another couple, friends of Mousie's. We all got on pretty well. Well, we had to, there wasn't all that much room. Mousie's friend's friend was pretty annoyed. Said he was going to complain to the agency. Kept taking photographs of the bathroom to prove that it was inadequate. I just made the best of it. It does one no harm to rough it from time to time.'

Blanche, who remembered Bertie as a man of the utmost fastidiousness, filling the bathroom with smells of verbena and sandalwood, marvelled at this, only saying, 'You are eating Patrick's pudding, Bertie.'

'So I am,' said Bertie, taking another small but crucial slice.

'I was thinking of going away for a bit myself,' said Blanche. 'I have been in the flat for what seems to me a very long time. I am not needed here.'

'What do you mean, Blanche, not needed?'

'I mean, Bertie, that no one would notice if I disappeared. It is, of course, delightful to see you again, and you too, Patrick, but I am sure that I am not essential to either of you. You both have other commitments. That leaves me quite free. I shall go south and sit in the sun. As Patrick and I have agreed, it is sometimes essential to please oneself. Nature tells us to.'

She began to put plates, knives, and forks on to the tray, having apparently decided that the meal was at an end. Patrick made a half-hearted attempt to help her, getting up from his chair, pushing his plate towards her. Having done this he sat down again.

'Of course,' said Blanche pleasantly, 'I can see that either of you might want to drop in from time to time. My hospitality, though modest, is profound. I shall never be guilty of saying that your visits are inconvenient. As a matter of fact they are not. I am not, as you must have noticed, excessively busy. But who is to say that I might not want to be somewhere else?'

'You invited me, Blanche,' said Patrick.

'So I did. That was only because we had something to discuss. But I was thinking of you, Bertie. You seem to expect me to be here all the time, just as I always was.'

'I came because Barbara told me you were ill. I wondered if you needed anything.'

'You wondered if I needed anything? How thoughtful. But as you see, I am, as I always was, self-sufficient. Oh, are you going, Patrick? Must you? I am suddenly feeling rather sociable.'

Patrick, looking grave, had picked up his briefcase. 'I will telephone you, Blanche, about the arrangements. You will want to know as soon as possible. And I do realize what I am doing, you know.'

'But he doesn't,' said Blanche to Bertie, as she came back into the room after seeing Patrick to the door. 'He looks so senatorial that one invests him with more wisdom than he could possibly possess. I was right to worry about him, all those years ago. I think I knew that something would always stop him making up his mind. And now he is in the grip of a great decision. It will be a defeat for him either way. Patrick's effectiveness stops short of action. Action is by now so foreign to him that it presents itself as a disaster. And he knows this in his heart of hearts. It is just that he is so tired of being safe. I do understand that.'

'You have apparently got to know him very well.'

'Have a drink, Bertie. I always knew him well. I knew how he suffered from his own shortcomings. As we all do. I wanted to make him feel safer than he knew how to feel on his own, safer than he *deserved* to feel. Perhaps it was silly of me. One shouldn't try to buttress people against the world. The gods are stronger than we are.'

'Blanche,' said Bertie.

'No, don't stop me. I have been thinking a great deal about the past and now I see it more clearly. You were bound to leave me, Bertie. I had served my term. The restlessness that drives men to folly drives them away from people like me. It was as futile for me to try to keep you as it would have been for me to try to turn myself into someone twenty years younger. And then I saw the pattern. The pattern is plain for all to see. One visit to the National Gallery would convince you, if you were in any doubt. There they all are, the good and the indifferent. I incline to think that there *are* no bad. Indifference to the good is all that is needed.'

'If you are alluding to Mousie, then you are wrong. Mousie is fundamentally a very good and caring person.'

'Mousie is a novice, Bertie. Mousie's weapons are a girl's weapons, crude. Basically she is rather timorous. Afraid of the wrath to come. Why else does she keep sending you round here to see if I have put my head in the gas oven? Why else does she need the approbation of her friends to keep her going? Why share a villa in Corfu when she could have had you to herself? No, Mousie is not a bad person. She is a child, defying her elders, and she is so charming that they do not slap her. But grown-up children can be very dangerous. Women who persist in thinking of themselves as little girls tend to think their misdemeanours unimportant. I have to say that they usually get away with it. You can open that other bottle if you want to. Patrick seems to have drunk most of the first. It is a sign of his agitation.'

'He looked pretty comfortable to me. And can't we talk about something else? Must I always do penance?'

'It is what you come here for, Bertie. And there is no need, you know. I have just been trying to explain to you. I see the pattern.'

'I do wish you'd shut up, occasionally, Blanche. You always did talk too much.'

'And you get less talk in Fulham?'

'It is of a different nature.'

'I can see that women drive men mad,' said Blanche, lighting a cigarette. 'What I can't see is why some of them get away with it.'

'No, I'm sure you can't. The corkscrew is by your elbow, if you wouldn't mind. I should just like to point out that I have done a hard day's work and that I should like a moment's peace and quiet.'

'Men always say that. I remember my father saying it. Have you eaten, by the way?'

'Only that piece of tart.'

Blanche went into the kitchen and came back with the rest of the jellied chicken, some buttered water biscuits, a piece of Wensleydale, and a peach. She assembled it all on a tray and put the tray on Bertie's knees. 'What were the arrangements that Patrick was talking about?' he asked, picking up his fork and darting a quick glance at her when she was not looking.

'Arrangements? Oh, the *arrangements*. Well, I rather think the arrangements are Patrick's affair.'

Watching Bertie eat, as she had done so many times, she was distressed to find that she felt the simple satisfactions of an earlier mode of being. It was as if, in him, she found intimations of her own validity, as if without him that validity disappeared. This was no way, she knew, for a self-respecting modern woman to feel. She also knew that his absence had driven her to strange excesses, all the more strange because they seemed so harmless. Just as some women turn to drink, to food, to shoplifting, Blanche had turned to flirtations with other lives, good works, and uplifting pastimes. She had never doubted that her heart was not fully engaged in these activities, but she had accepted them, haplessly and with a feeling of humility, apologizing all the while to older and more vigorous memories of her former self, for her abject impersonation of worthiness, trying, without prejudice, to learn the art of self-sufficiency. She, who had called Mousie timorous, had become even more timorous herself, able to recognize in others the panic fight for freedom, able to appreciate, to admire, what she now thought of as indifference. For although her place was here, her services must be devoted elsewhere, whatever the misconceptions involved, whatever the misalliances, and despite the clouded conscience that came from an awareness that she was, in all this, without enthusiasm. Bertie, glancing at her over his fork, saw that she looked stern, mysterious.

'What are you thinking?' he asked politely, knowing that

this was the sort of question to which she always, and voluminously, responded.

'I was thinking of other lives,' she said, 'and how attractive they always look. And how misleading they are when you know a little more about them. It is probably better to leave other lives alone. And I suppose I was thinking about children and how they present you with a version of yourself. Or how you feel yourself to be.'

But this was of no interest to Bertie, who at last came round to what was uppermost in his mind.

'What will you do about Patrick?' he said.

'About Patrick? Why should I do anything about Patrick?'

'I got the impression that you and he were going away together.'

Blanche laughed. 'How little you know him. If there were any question of Patrick going away with me he'd be busy discussing it with somebody else. You surely can't think, Bertie ...'

'Well, yes,' he said stiffly. 'I did rather.'

'And how little you know *me*. If I went away with anyone it would hardly be with Patrick. I should choose someone with a little more, how shall I put it? *Élan? Élan vital?* Patrick is *decorous*. Do you remember how my mother approved of him for just that reason? Patrick might well go overboard for a woman but it would hardly be for someone like me.'

'Why not? You are still attractive.'

'But don't you understand? Patrick sees *me* as decorous. Someone who can be relied upon to do the decent thing.' She laughed again. 'And if only you knew how tired I am of doing the decent thing. Or trying to do it.' She gestured out of the window. 'There are people out there, Bertie, who never do the decent thing. You know them. I know them. I used to think that I could spot them all over the place. I blame the National Gallery for that, of course. All those deities carrying on their uninhibited lives. *In full view*. It took me a long time to realize that anyone can do it, if they have a mind to. I still don't know whether it takes will or just capacity. The character of such lives is to be unfinished, open-ended, escaping control. I suppose that is what gives them their mythic quality. Others abide our question; they are apparently free.'

'Then who will you go away with?'

'Oh, I don't know, I don't know. Maybe I shall go alone and make the best of it. My pleasures are very simple, as you know. It will not be a holiday like the one you have just had. There will be no crowd to make up a party for dinner. I enjoyed it once. I suppose you still do.'

'I like company, yes.'

'And I expect,' she said lightly, looking out of the window, 'that you and Mousie will get married one of these days.'

'I dare say we shall get around to it.'

There was a silence, for this, to Blanche, was the end of everything. He watched her carefully. 'When will you go?' he said.

'Oh, as soon as possible. There are one or two things to be sorted out here, one or two involvements, and then I shall go. I might even look for somewhere to live. I think that might be best. Yes, that is what I shall do. You can have this flat, of course. You always liked it more than I did.'

'You seem to find it very easy to get rid of our past life.'

'I do, don't I? Perhaps I should have done it earlier. I have been ridiculous, sitting here, waiting for you to come. And telling you not to. As if that were any way to live. Plato tells us that pleasures mixed with pain are only lesser pleasures. How right he is.'

'Is that all I am? One of the lesser pleasures?'

'What you are can no longer be serious, because it is half-hearted. Your life is somewhere else, somewhere inaccessible to me. One is supposed to get over these things, and I shall get over it, of course I shall. It is just taking rather a long time, that's all. And I dare say I am to blame. At the moment my life is no longer serious either. I am playing at being something that I do not know properly how to be. And I shall see it through to the end because honour is the highest good. I believe that to be true. But how hard it is, sometimes. How I should like to be different.'

'Don't change, Blanche.'

'I think I must, you know. I will hardly do as I am; my respectability is against me. I have cast myself for the wrong role. Well, it is too late to do anything about that. As I say, I shall see it through. But then I shall try to change. Try to live a little more carelessly. Artlessly. That is to say, without art. Art can be very subversive. I have found that out.'

'I must go,' he said, glancing at his watch.

'Yes,' she replied. 'You must.'

'Your standards were always too high, Blanche.'

'Were they? Then they will have to go too.'

She got up and started straightening cushions. He caught her arm, but she turned away.

'I never was, you know,' he said, turning away himself.

'Never was what?'

'Half-hearted,' he said.

That night Blanche stood at the window, curtain in hand, watching the street. Then she went to bed and lay for a long time, unsleeping.

TWELVE

'Had quite a party here last night, I see,' said Miss Elphinstone, turning on both taps and speaking above the noise. 'Mind you don't go overdoing it, now. You don't look at all well to me.'

'I'm going away,' said Blanche, feeling like Captain Oates. 'I might be gone for some time.'

Nothing surprised Miss Elphinstone. Trained in the ways of the Lord, she was proof against all contingencies, although strangely indifferent to life's more savage demonstrations. Routinely cheerful, she could be thought by the unwary to be complacent, were it not for her smile, which flashed on and off unpredictably; sometimes Blanche would attempt to cut short Miss Elphinstone's elaborate marginalia only to be rewarded by a smile of great benevolence which revealed, if anything, a consciousness greatly superior to her own. Miss Elphinstone, upright and blameless, unchanging in her demeanour and her attributes, was a tribune of excellence before which Blanche was obliged to lay all her plans. Nothing was really tolerable without Miss Elphinstone's approval. It was Miss Elphinstone who had cast doubt on Blanche's attempts to entertain Elinor, saying that Elinor was too young to go out without her mother. Since that remark, Blanche had looked askance at her own efforts and had distanced herself from her earlier eagerness. Part of her reluctance to admit Sally to the flat stemmed from a sense of Miss Elphinstone's disapproval, although this was not the entire story. On her only visit Sally's appraising eye had been quick to compute the difference in income between Blanche and herself and had pitched her expectations accordingly; those expectations had been relentless but not on the whole unreasonable. Now that she was leaving, Blanche desired to put the record straight on as many counts as possible. A great movement of renovation was under way for which she must be worthy. She submitted to Miss Elphinstone her need for a change of air and was oddly relieved to see her nod in agreement. 'Well, I've got my key,' she said. 'I'll look in same as usual. I expect you'll turn up again when you've had enough. Do you want to take that dish next door to Mrs Duff before you forget?' For to Miss Elphinstone, the immediate task was more interesting than the remote possibility; it could be said that she had little imagination were it not for her sense of priorities, which safeguarded her against eccentricity. Miss Elphinstone was demonstrably sane, without fantasies; great was her interest in other lives, yet by some sort of divine sanction she was immune to any effect they might have had on her own. Blanche envied her her impermeability: having no sense of the relative importance or unimportance of others, Miss Elphinstone lived a life of true enlightenment, always mildly interested but never ill-served by curiosity, and virtuously immune to speculation. Miss Elphinstone would allow Blanche a certain leeway in her affairs though she would be quick to notice anomalies. She appeared to think that a short absence could be sanctioned. Blanche did not tell her by how much the absence might be prolonged, for she was not yet clear about this in her own mind. She thought in terms of reconnaissance, of looking for a house. But really she felt it was her removal from this place that counted, rather than her presence elsewhere, for she saw that presence as nebulous, immaterial. She allowed her mind to rest on the fact that

Miss Elphinstone saw her need to get away; what was to happen next was as yet without definition and could be kept at bay for the time being.

It was a beautiful soft day, of the kind that announces autumn. An early sun had given way to a whitish grey clarity, against which the dark trees stood immobile in the windless air. Outside the greengrocer's ragged asters and tight complicated dahlias had taken the place of the unconvincing roses and carnations of a metropolitan summer. Leaves, although still green, were beginning to fall; a man was sweeping them from the gutters. Blanche made her way for the last time to Sally's basement; some impulse caused her to buy a bunch of flowers, the sort of greeting that Sally might find appropriate, for it was somehow unthinkable to appear before her empty-handed. Sally received presents; she did not give them. Blanche's cakes, and even her money, she saw now, were disdained as graceless. Sally preferred funds to come winging through the atmosphere, preferably in large quantities, without the embarrassment of a known human intermediary. Thus, while accepting all contributions, she would deplore the style of the giver, and in so doing, remain faithful to her own standards. Blanche began to see that Sally had never cast herself as a deserving or a needy case; she merely thought it reasonable that others should tide her over, until a throw of the dice should have moved her on to a different state of affairs. Theoretically she was always willing to do the same for others, but practically this was somehow never possible. While recounting past generosities and affirming future ones Sally was always in the present without funds. To Sally, accountability was the sign of a pinched and feeble spirit. Yet she implied criticism of those who did not help her, as if she had taken rapid and expert measure of their financial position.

It occurred to Blanche that she had been wildly anachronistic in trying to impose reasonable expectations on Sally.

Sally's expectations, she now knew, were so different from her own as to seem incomprehensible, just as she, Blanche, had seemed incomprehensible to Sally. 'You do so little,' Sally had once said, meaning, 'You do so little with your money,' for although she asked no questions she possessed accurate information. Her instincts were so untrammelled that her view of things was in an odd way right. Not for her the hesitations of reflection, the pale cast of thought. What she would have appreciated was some huge treat, since in her view Blanche was in a position to offer her one, a shopping spree, the gift of a car, or a holiday. Anything less met with clouded indifference and a look of disappointment, as if she detected the giver in an attitude of unworthiness. Silence was her only answer to Blanche's contributions although she never hesitated to solicit them. Indeed, her reaction was to solicit more, as if hoping to stimulate Blanche to some vast final disgorgement of funds, upon receipt of which she would, at last, smile.

It was difficult to fault her, thought Blanche, sniffing the scentless crimson dahlias. There was no blame attaching: it was just that in her dealings with Sally misconceptions ruled. Those misconceptions had been complicated. On a reasonable level she had truly expected only to tide Sally over, as she put it. But superimposed on this had been the fascination of an alien species, one that literally took no heed of the morrow, and passed through life expecting pleasures where others would think in terms of duties. The irregularity of Sally's life, the contrast between past affluence and present indigence, the promising information, which turned out not be information at all, the complicated situation of the husband, the misreading of the character of the Demuths and of their durability – as if they were not expected to outlast her acquaintance with them – and above all the obduracy of the child, which now seemed less emblematic, less symbolic, and more a symptom of late but normal development: all this she had cast in the form of a story to which she might contribute. The essence of the story, however, was not that she was expected to help it along but merely to read it, in instalments, supplying appropriate exclamations of wonder, indignation, encouragement, sympathy. If she had been needed at all it was as a chorus, discreetly unfolding money in a suitably bodiless and unembarrassing manner, and contributing an uncritical appreciation of Sally's current difficulties. That no single human being could maintain this attitude indefinitely did not matter to Sally; after all, there were plenty of others, all of them replaceable. The essential thing was to be Sally, but here Blanche saw that she was overstating the case, for Sally had never once stepped outside her own consciousness. If Mr Demuth refused Paul money, then Mr Demuth was a beast, a vile, crass, ignorant primitive. Of Mrs Demuth she appeared to have no clear picture, probably because she found it hard to credit other women with their own identity. Mrs Demuth was simply someone who was storing her fur coat. Whether she knew of its true ownership Blanche had no idea, probably not, for she had always thought of it as hers. Patrick and Blanche she saw as dreary guardians of the constitution, pedantic in their attempts to sort out her affairs, although Patrick had shown promise in trying to step outside his role. But Sally knew that Patrick could not sustain his flight. Blanche she saw quite clearly as incapable of any flight whatsoever.

To be called to account, constantly, was Blanche's weakness; not to be called to account was Sally's strength. Looking through the smeared windows of the basement, Blanche was unsurprised to see a number of suitcases open on the green carpet, and in the middle of them Elinor, in blue trousers and a white anorak, playing with a variety of toys that Blanche had not noticed before. Her little basket chair was upended in a corner; on a plate on the trolley lay a half-eaten slice of toast. Going down the steps, Blanche realized that once again her contribution was mistimed and misplaced: the flowers would be laid aside, and, when she had gone, thrown away. Plans had been made, but no information imparted. Information, of a remotely relevant order, had been omitted all along, yet Blanche did not now, did no longer, attempt to extract it. She had come to announce that she was going away, and saw no reason why the formalities should be prolonged. Later that day she would see the bank manager and her solicitor and make financial arrangements for Elinor, and after that she was free, free to make her own arrangements and to disappear, possibly for ever. Speed now seemed to her the essence of the undertaking.

Sally greeted her with a look of slight surprise, as if she expected her already to have vanished. Gesturing to her empty suitcases, she said, 'You don't mind if I go on packing, do you? Only some friends are calling for me at twelve.'

'You're leaving?' said Blanche, stepping over a little cart with a toy poodle in it.

'We're leaving, thank God. Nellie's going to grandmama and I'm going on holiday.'

'On holiday? What fun,' she added hastily, recalling the appropriate response.

'Isn't it? A friend of ours from the old days tracked me down. I'm going to his house in Cornwall. God knows I need a break.'

'Yes, I'm sure you do,' said Blanche, mindful of the note to be struck. 'Paul must be pleased.' She noticed a large bunch of roses, dying from dehydration, in an elaborate crystal vase.

'Paul must sort out his own affairs. I've told him where I'll be. Then when he gets rid of those awful people he can come and join us. There's no point in my hanging around here.'

This was tantamount to a great deal of information. 'Did he tell you what had been decided?' Blanche asked.

Sally glanced at her. 'They're going back to America. Well, you know that, of course. I can't be expected to wait around for him.' She seemed to bear a grudge for Blanche's intervention, as if Blanche alone had been responsible for Mr Demuth's decision. 'God knows what you said to them,' she added.

'I tried to explain ...' Blanche began, but gave up. 'It might have been better if you hadn't asked me to intervene,' she couldn't help remarking. 'I thought it was a bad idea, if you remember.'

'Well, it doesn't matter now, does it? At least you saw what we were up against. Not that that helps me much.' She turned her back and devoted herself to the folding of a long red silk skirt. Blanche bent down to Elinor and handed her the bunch of flowers, which Elinor laid in her cart.

'Did you see Daddy?' she asked. Elinor nodded her head firmly. Blanche was surprised. 'Did Paul come here?' she asked Sally. There had been no word of this.

'Oh, no,' said Sally, closing a suitcase. 'We went there. He gave us lunch at the Dorchester. Not bad. Nellie loved it. She's started to speak, by the way.'

'Why, Elinor,' said Blanche, with a great feeling of joy. 'What a clever girl. Can you say my name? Can you say Blanche?' Elinor nodded firmly once again but remained silent. Oh, well, thought Blanche. This is worth a great deal. It is, after all, a sort of happy ending. At the same time she was surprised that Sally's indifference had not modulated into something more positive; in fact, with her increased activity, she seemed to be getting more bad-tempered, as if obstacles were being put in her way, or as if she had finally lost patience with those who had, at any time, attempted to impede her. This flight of hers, Blanche saw, might be another stage in her eternal mobility; since she obviously did not plan to come back, it was clear that somewhere else must be found for her, and the implication was that this task would be left to others. The friends who were coming to collect her at twelve, the friend from the old days who had lent his house in Cornwall, might be obliged to harbour Sally until further plans were improvised. She would not reappear in this place, in this context; this stage of her life was now over, as was the time in which she had lent herself to the nurture of Elinor, who would now pass into the care of her grandmother. By the same token, Paul could be discarded with no blame attaching. 'It just didn't work out,' Blanche could hear Sally saying, and Paul would disappear, dematerialize, leaving no trace behind. And all these necessary plans had been made in the space of a few days, more evidence, if evidence were needed, of Sally's magical thinking.

'I'm so glad I caught you,' said Blanche. 'I came to say goodbye. I'm going away myself.'

'Oh, yes,' said Sally, over her shoulder.

'Yes,' Blanche repeated. 'I may be gone for some time.'

Sally straightened up. 'In that case, what's going to happen to your flat?'

'My flat?'

'Yes. Will there be anyone in it?'

Blanche stared at her, then burst out laughing.

Sally appeared to be offended. 'I only thought ... Well, if we get stuck. I don't know what you're laughing at. Have I said something funny?'

Blanche's laughter, which surprised her, also liberated her from the thrall of this particular situation. Suddenly, there was no need to feel anything at all. She bent down and kissed Elinor. 'Goodbye, darling,' she said. 'Have a lovely time. Goodbye, Sally.'

'Goodbye,' said Sally, reverting to her usual indifference.

'By the way,' said Blanche, turning at the door. 'What did she say when she spoke?'

'Oh, I don't know,' said Sally. 'Something about Grandma. Going to Grandma. Something like that. I forget.'

So even that historic moment had passed without due recognition. Her last sight of Sally was of a figure bending over a suitcase, carefully folding in her expensive multicoloured garments: in this, as in all other matters of presentation, she could not be faulted.

Looking back at the door, as she so often had before, Blanche saw them both busy, turned away from her. Quite suddenly, and without warning, she realized that they were irrelevant to her, and she to them. She was just as easily aware that she should have seen this before: disaster had made her incompetent. The inscrutable child was still inscrutable to her, the mother just as foreign. She had made no difference to them. As always, but with less passion than previously, she blamed herself. To have assumed that she could love them and make them love her was more than folly: it was an error. To have assumed a bond between Elinor and herself was more serious a fault. The child was not hers to love. That was still a surprise. And the child somehow knew this. The wisdom of Elinor's instincts amazed her into an admiration that was no less genuine for having been glimpsed, imperfectly, before, in other circumstances. As for herself, she had made her usual mistakes, thinking love to be easy, sweet, natural, reposeful, understood. Just as she had thought that love, once reciprocated – the child's hand in hers – could be counted as a blessed state, without thoughts of possession. I was foolish, she thought. They saw my attempts at love as misappropriation. The full force of this truth struck her with incredulity, stupefaction. It was a misalliance, she thought. I have never fully understood the laws of property. If I had, I should not be alone, at this moment, and apparently forced to remain so.

But being so forced, she let her needs and desires drop away from her, and blowing the child a kiss (which the child did not see) she let herself out of the door, turning almost eagerly to the clear light, away from the musty room to the soft sun of autumn. Walking back through the agreeable, obligation-free streets, she found her mood growing ever more expansive, irresponsible. Bubbles of laughter escaped her from time to time. On an impulse, she went into the hairdresser's and had most of her hair cut off. This symbolic action seemed to demand others. Airily she made her way to the hospital and told the people in the office that she would not be coming in for some time. 'For how long?' asked the Senior Nursing Officer. 'Only we like to know where we are.'

'Well, I think for quite a long while,' said Blanche.

'It's just that we like to know who will be here for the Christmas period. And we couldn't do without *you*, Mrs Vernon. Always so reliable.'

Perhaps you will have to, thought Blanche, as they parted with warm smiles on both sides. After that, there seemed a lot to do, but the weather was so beguiling that she delayed going back to the flat, where she must write many necessary letters, and preferred to saunter in the mild air, looking at shop windows, buying the first blackberries, and more dahlias, for herself, this time. Then, carefully, she selected a magnificent gloxinia, its trumpet flowers shading from deep crimson down to white throats, for Mrs Duff. She determined to spend the afternoon discarding what she thought of as her National Gallery clothes, which Miss Elphinstone could certainly wear, if only she could be persuaded not to give them to the church jumble sale, and putting her affairs in order. One suitcase was all that she would take, and anything she needed could be bought *en route*. These decisions made her feel literally weightless. 'Lorraine,' she said, putting her head round the door of the local travel agent's. 'Can you get me on a flight to Paris the day after tomorrow? I'll call back later.' Then, almost regretfully, she went home.

The flat seemed dark in comparison with the bright day outside. Perhaps it was. Perhaps it always had been. She stripped the bed, wanting for these last two nights to sleep in immaculate sheets. Walking past her dressing-table, she was surprised by her new appearance: the mournful lines had vanished, along with most of her hair. Interested, she applied make-up, turned her head this way and that, put a dubious hand to the nape of her neck. All seemed to be in order. She changed into a dark purple linen dress, the colour that the blackberries would be when mixed with cream, and, taking the gloxinia and the dish, went next door to Mrs Duff. This acquaintance, to which she had been so long indifferent, now seemed to present itself in the same mellow colours as the day. She would not forget that deep compassionate look, that succouring arm, for many years, nor did she intend to. Fiercely disciplined, and long inured to dealing with herself, ill or well, she looked back in wonder to the moment of her rescue. She thought it probable that her new lightness had its roots in that moment.

'Oh, you look lovely,' said Mrs Duff, ushering her into a room identical to her own but much brighter. This was no doubt due to Mrs Duff's taste in decoration, which expressed itself in terms of love seats and embroidered rugs and a crowd of Staffordshire figures. The walls were covered in a handsome yellow grosgrain which set off the darker gold of the carpet. In a large brass jardinière, dazzlingly polished, was assembled a flourishing collection of fleshy green plants. Thick white Nottingham lace curtains hung from brass rails and were looped back at the windows. From this uncompromising apartment Mrs Duff had wrested a Victorian cottage. Blanche expressed her delighted admiration. 'Oh, but you must see our bedroom,' beamed Mrs Duff. 'I was going to redecorate it but my husband told me not to change a thing. He loves it. And it *is* comfortable.' It was more than comfortable; it was seductive. It was also redolent of the deep peace of the double bed. White flowers twined over the walls on a blue ground; deep blue carpet covered the floor and a thick white chenille counterpane the bed. Under an ottoman covered in blue and white stripes were placed two pairs of slippers, both red. At the head of the bed, on two white tables, curved two milk glass lamps on brass stems, their globes shaped like the flowers of the gloxinia. A modest tube of hand cream indicated Mrs Duff's side of the bed. 'We made the second bedroom into a dressing-room,' she explained, throwing open another door on to a room done in blue and white stripes, with white louvred wardrobes and a long looking-glass on a stand. 'A psyche, those used to be called,' she said. 'It came from Mother's workroom. Yes,' she went on, 'we meant this room to be something different. But there it is. I mustn't go on. And it's not too late for coffee, is it? I've just made some almond biscuits.' For there was, predictably, a fine smell of baking.

Seated on a small plump sofa, Blanche told Mrs Duff of her plans and met with her entire approval. 'I'll keep the key,' she said, 'and make sure that everything's all right.' Blanche felt safe in the other woman's care, and at the same time felt she had been granted licence to try her wings. For no one could tell what this journey would bring, or even whether she would come home again. This knowledge made the present day seem like a holiday, agreeably temporary, soon to vanish, along with the entire scenery of her life as she knew it. She had a vision of flying railway lines, narrowing, crossing, diverging again, and of herself on some wayside station in the very early morning, sniffing the thyme-scented air. For the moment, taking coffee in this parlour had the charm of novelty, as did every detail of Mrs Duff's appearance: her cream-coloured skirt and her dark blue blouse and the very small coffee-coloured shoes into which her astonishingly highly arched feet nestled. 'You have a dancer's feet,' said Blanche, and Mrs Duff delightedly confessed that she loved dancing and had thought she might take it up as a career, had it not been for the sight, when she was sixteen years old, of her future husband, and her determination to marry him, forged in that significant moment. 'He didn't know, of course.' Out of the window went her plans to dance on the London stage, and she helped out Mother in the showroom, simply biding her time until she judged it seemly to accept John's proposal, and all the while putting away quantities of fine linen, so that their first home should lack none of the niceties. A white wedding, of course, and all the trimmings. And never a cross word since. Mind you, a woman had to know how to handle men, how to make them feel comfortable. Once you knew how to do that you could deal with any little problems that might arise. Mrs Duff was of the opinion that all men were little boys at heart. Blanche nodded, entranced by this view of human affairs and by the firmness with which Mrs Duff delivered it. Her sapphire ring sparkled on her fine white hand as she lifted Blanche's cup and poured into it a fragrant stream of excellent coffee. Blanche had expected the coffee to be weak – her own was always too strong – but the beautiful decorum of Mrs Duff's household management confounded her expectations. A shaft of sun struck through the window, as an almond biscuit, essence of bourgeois sweetness, crumbled into sugary dust on Blanche's tongue.

It was after leaving the bright room, and after taking her leave of Mrs Duff, that the first tremor of melancholy made itself felt. The sun, bright now over the quiet streets, drew Blanche to her window, and she stood for some time in her familiar attitude, with her hand holding back the curtain. She realized how long it had taken for the sun to gain its ascendancy on this particular day and, remembering the uncertain light of the morning, the windless air, the black-berries, and the dahlias, knew that this was truly autumn. The evening would be a short one; darkness would come early. And soon a harvest moon, the moon that was nearly golden. She would miss all that, of course, for she would be where the sun shone all day. With a sigh, which she did not hear, she moved resolutely to her desk and sat down to pay bills and to write letters, notes for the milkman and the laundryman, a note cancelling the papers, an envelope containing Miss Elphinstone's money until the end of the year, together with the rigidly itemized account on which Miss Elphinstone insisted. She telephoned Barbara and said she would let her have an address as soon as she arrived, would in fact telephone as soon as she arrived. 'But where will you be?' asked Barbara anxiously, and, 'Is this wise, Blanche?'

'It is more than wise; it is necessary,' Blanche replied, and she supposed that it was. After putting the receiver down she took out a suitcase and started to pack.

With the waning of the sun came the full melancholy, the melancholy of departure. She was a decisive woman and her preparations had not taken her long. She made an omelette with herbs which she would eat later, cold, with some garlic bread and the rest of the blackberries. After that there seemed very little to do. She roamed restlessly round the flat, checking her dressing-table, draping a sweater round her shoulders, pushing her suitcase out of sight. It was a relief to sit down with a bottle of Frascati, although this evening the wine was not to her taste. She was too agitated to sit quietly and thought of going for a long walk, tiring herself out, and thus ensuring a night's sleep. For tomorrow she must pick up her ticket and take her leave, so that on the following day she could disappear silently, without witnesses. In the event she doubted whether it would be as seamless a departure as she had recently imagined it to be, but she put this down to an unusual form of nervousness, brought on by her long reclusion from the world, and tried not to let the fear take hold.

It took hold, none the less, and she went early to bed, by now more than willing to enter the world of night, in which only the action of dreams was possible. A certain formality helped to keep misgivings at bay, and she dressed in her best nightgown, which had been laid in a drawer for over a year. With a sigh she got into bed, took up her book, and prepared to read for an hour, but after a few minutes the book fell from her hand, and her head turned to the window. There was nothing to see now, and no sound to be heard. She listened in vain for the cat with the bell round its neck, padding along on its night-time patrol. Straining her ears she heard not the sound of the cat's bell but of the front door: a key had been inserted cautiously into the lock. For an insane moment she imagined herself pursued by the entire Beamish family – Sally, Paul, Elinor, the grandmother – each member of which had somehow managed to furnish itself with a key. She sat up in bed with a wildly beating heart until she realized that this was impossible, that her visitor could only be Mrs Duff or Miss Elphinstone, about her parochial business at the hospital and looking in as she had promised. 'Is that you, Miss Elphinstone?' she called out. There was no answer. 'Mrs Duff?' she said, in a voice from which conviction was dwindling. There was a noise of keys being dropped, and then her bedroom door slowly opened.

'I'm back, Blanche,' said Bertie, putting down a suitcase. 'I've come back. What have you done to your hair?'

Anita Brookner is the author of the best-selling *Hotel du Lac* as well as the novels *A Start in Life*, *Providence*, *Look at Me*, and *Family and Friends*. An international authority on eighteenth-century painting, Brookner teaches at the Courtauld Institute of Art and has also written *Watteau*, *The Genius of the Future*, *Greuze*, and *Jacques-Louis David*.